ONCE in a
BLUE MOON

ONCE in a
BLUE MOON

SHARON G. FLAKE

ALFRED A. KNOPF · NEW YORK

THIS IS A BORZOI BOOK PUBLISHED BY ALFRED A. KNOPF

Visit us on the Web! rhcbooks.com

Educators and librarians, for a variety of teaching tools, visit us at RHTeachersLibrarians.com

Library of Congress Cataloging-in-Publication Data
Names: Flake, Sharon G., author.
Title: Once in a blue moon / Sharon G. Flake.
Description: First edition. | New York : Alfred A. Knopf, [2023] | Audience: Ages 8–12. | Audience: Grades 4–6. | Summary: Paralyzed by guilt, eleven-year-old John Henry must come to terms with the events surrounding his Ma's near drowning and, with the help of his twin sister Hattie, learn to embrace life again.
Identifiers: LCCN 2022053057 (print) | LCCN 2022053058 (ebook) | ISBN 978-0-593-48098-4 (hardcover) | ISBN 978-0-593-48099-1 (library binding) | ISBN 978-0-593-48100-4 (ebook)
Subjects: CYAC: Novels in verse. | Psychic trauma—Fiction. | Guilt—Fiction. | Twins—Fiction. | Siblings—Fiction. | Bullies and bullying—Fiction. | Friendship—Fiction. | African Americans—Fiction. | LCGFT: Novels in verse.
Classification: LCC PZ7.5.F58 On 2023 (print) | LCC PZ7.5.F58 (ebook) | DDC [Fic]—dc23

Photo on page 324 courtesy of the author
The text of this book is set in 11.75-point Adobe Garamond Pro.
Interior design by Michelle Crowe

Printed in the United States of America
10 9 8 7 6 5 4 3 2 1
First Edition

For my father—the boy he was and the man he became—
thank you for never giving up and always looking up.

ONCE in a
BLUE MOON

PART 1

TROUBLES

ME

People ask about the boy
behind the door
inside the house
me.
Mostly Sister gets the questions.
She chases away boys
girls too sometimes
who wander onto our property
to gawk and stare at me
the one
folks hardly see
but everybody knows about.

ME AND SISTER

Hattie and me are twins
not that we match exactly.

She's two inches taller
I'm two minutes older
a boy.
Eleven
though I seem younger.
Maybe that's why Hattie likes to boss me around.
But I'm the captain
        today anyhow.
Which means
she's got to follow my rules.

MY CONDITION

Sometimes
I feel as small as a flea
as little as the space between
the numbers on a watch.

It makes living hard
staying inside easier than leaving the house.

Right now
I'm on my knees
on the couch
by the window
staring out—like usual.

Hattie's
to the right of the porch
next to the gravel walkway
in front of the bushes Gran asked her to trim
  yesterday.

It's a boy's job
my job
but given my condition
Hattie gets to take my place
more than I'd like
not that I like
toting pails
feeding chickens
milking.

THE WAY THINGS ARE

We live in Seed County, North Carolina.
Daddy is in Detroit
working.
Here, it's me
Gran
and Hattie in the house.
Uncle comes by now and again.

He don't like me much.

HATTIE'S WAY

How many times you got to call
a girl before she answers?

One time?
        Two times?
                Ten?

"Hattie Mae!" I say again.

Outside past the porch
she squats low
picks up a rope
that came from Detroit
wrapped around a box of new dresses
        sent to her by Daddy.

She holds both ends
        swings
that rope
        over her head
jumps
HIGH
sends dirt flying.

Still
she ignores me.

Could be she's mad at me.
This is the third time this week I said
I'd go outside
try to anyhow.

Only I can't.

SISTER'S SONG

Sister is dressed for Sunday
when it's only Wednesday.
She sings while she jumps
hops
skips.
"Miss Mary Mack, Mack, Mack . . ."

But as soon as her song starts
it stops.

"Everybody's got a condition," she says.
"Pastor wheezes when he preaches.
Sneezes come spring.
Still
he gets out the house."

I get out
at night, at least.
If folks looked up, there I'd be
on the roof
under the sky
talking to Hattie
the only one allowed up there
besides me.

My rules
even when I'm not the captain.

LIGHTHOUSES AND BLUE MOONS

Sister takes her sweet time walking
up the pine front-porch steps
sawed and nailed in place by Granddad, who built the house.

Halfway between the porch and me
    she stops
gives Gran a hug
reminds her that there'll be
a blue moon in a few months' time.

Who don't know that?

The almanac calls
the second full moon in a month
a blue moon.
It don't happen too often.
Which makes it a big deal
important
unusual.

Gran calls it a wishing moon.
What you want for, wish for
or need
on that day is yours
according to her.

Which is why Hattie is nagging me so.
If I'm to be rid of my condition
she believes
we need to get to the ocean
on the night of the blue moon
get to the lighthouse too
where I was when everything changed.

Which means
    I have to get out of this house first.

Only I can't.
Why don't folks understand that?

Ma would.

HATTIE IN THE HOUSE

Hattie comes inside
when I say I don't feel so well.

Sister swears it's nothing.
Just me worrying
or about to.
Still
she puts her hand on my forehead.

Feels like something.

Needles poke my legs.
Fire burns my toes and fingernails.
My insides
hum
like guitar strings just plucked.

It's my nerves
playing tricks on me
Doc Edwards claimed
during his once-a-month visit.

Feels like something worse.

"Hattie," Gran says from where she sits rocking
on the porch,
"leave him be."

Hattie stands behind me.
Hugs me.
Brings up Doc Edwards.

I shiver
get cold to the bone.

My worrying is a worry to my soul
brain
blood and everything that makes
me
me
Doc Edwards said before he left town for good.

"Get him outside in the sun.
Drag him if you must," he told Daddy
not long after the accident
plus a few more times besides.

Daddy never did. Never would.
He understands me good as Ma.

MA'S TWIN

Uncle said
it was a fool's errand
that sent me to the ocean that night
with Ma chasing after me.

MORE ABOUT UNCLE

Uncle
never did trust up-north
big-city
fast-talking
pointy-toed-shoe-wearing folk
   Negro or white
not even Daddy at first.

Till Ma introduced him to Daddy's cousin Sarah.
She's our cousin and our aunt now.
They married ten years ago.
Got no kids
just each other plus a big white house.

Uncle came back south when Gran got sick.
Ma followed.
For just a spell they both said.
Then he got a job with the railroad.
Ma started teaching.

Six-two
pecan brown
Uncle dresses in clothes plain as paper bags.
Brown
brown
always brown.
His car is fancy, though.
His house has three floors. He built it himself.
Some nights I stayed with them. He liked me then.

MA

If it wasn't for Ma
I would believe what people say about me
that I'm peculiar
   odd
      a coward.

That night
Ma called me brave
   strong
      her little man
the smartest boy in Seed County.
I never told anybody that.

ROOFTOP

On my back
on top the roof
laying on a blanket
with my toes aimed at the sky
I forget my troubles.

The moon lights up the night.
Lights me up inside
fills me up
calms me down.
Hattie too.

Sister is nearby with her birds.

Standing in front of cages
stacked wide and high
Hattie looks after her treasures
doves
that think they're hawks.
Twelve in all.

Only Nutcracker is free right now.

ABOVE MY HEAD

Nutcracker flaps his wings
heads for his favorite spot
a chicken-wire fence Daddy put around the roof
    so we don't fall off.

Hattie sets another dove free
then another
till
there's ten of us on the roof
one complaining—
me.

The others coo
peck at seeds
corn kernels
dry peas
that Hattie scatters
in the cages
on the roof
and me.

I close my eyes again
think about Buck Rogers
    who is nothing like me.
Full-grown
white
he lives in the twenty-fifth century
    five hundred years in the future.

Ray guns.
Starships.
High-frequency impulses.

I never heard of such things
before his radio show.

Uncle doesn't like it one bit.
Says Buck and me
do the devil's work
by meditating on places
God never wanted folk to go
Venus
Neptune
Pluto
the Milky Way
the moon.

When I think on them
and other things above
I don't fear anything.

NIGHT TRAINS

The train runs along the track
    behind our house.
Black
spitting steam
it heads this way
on its way to the station.
Hattie's birds squawk and swoop.
I
pretend
I'm in first class
on my way to Sirius.

CAPTAIN ME

Hattie sits beside me
in a rain barrel I sawed in half.

I check the controls—
buttons and knobs
whittled out of wood
hammered
and
nailed into place with my very own hands.

Sister shifts gears using an old ax handle she swings in the air.

"Ready?" I ask.

Sister salutes.
"Aye, aye, Captain."

"Head protector?" I ask.

She pats her helmet
Gran's old church hat covered in tinfoil.
"Check," she says.

"Rocket fuel?"

Sister lifts a seltzer bottle full of well water.
"Enough for a month, sir."

"Jet pack?"

"Yes sir."

We got suspenders strapped on our backs
stitched to feed sacks filled with dried peas
handmade by Gran.

Hattie Mae licks her baby finger.
Holds it high.
"Good news, James Henry. Yesterday's storm
did not excite the wind too much.
We should make it to Neptune in record time
        without being blown off course."

I bolt the cabin door shut. "Ready?"

"Set," Hattie says.

"Blast off!" we scream.

The train rolls by.
Houses rumble and shake
including ours.
Smoke from the engine nearly blinds us.
Still
I see coloreds and whites on different planets.
Neptune not that far away.

TO OUTER SPACE AND BEYOND

"Space rocks!" Hattie Mae hollers at the top of her lungs.

Her birds know their parts.
Most times they stay in their cages
but before we got started she set 'em free
eight of 'em anyhow.

Pullman circles the roof—
Squawk!—
dives down
grabs buttons with his claws
drops 'em on us.

Aberdeen
     named after Ma
goes for the acorns.
Other birds pick up sticks
just like Sister trained 'em.

Our anti-radiation tinfoil hats
get hit from every which direction.
It doesn't hurt us any.
It's our rocket ship that's damaged.

The engine cuts off.
     "Ssssssss," Sister says.

The cabin light follows.
Birds go back in their cages.

In the dark
without power
we drift off course—like Buck Rogers.

Down
down
down
our spaceship goes
till we're in a part of the universe
we never saw before.

Sister pulls out a flashlight.
   The head is covered with cheesecloth.
Light rays shoot from it like sun through fog.

"It's . . . so empty out here. Quiet," I say.

Sister screams, "Aliens!"

I zap their tentacles with cow's milk.
Point to our instruments spinning out of control.

Hattie grabs her throat. Coughs. "We're losing oxygen. . . .
I . . . I'm dying . . . James Henry."

She faints
the way them movie stars do at the picture show
flopping over the side of the rocket ship
     eyes crossed.

I stand up. "I . . . won't . . . fail . . . you . . . Sister!"

"Oh goodness," I hear Gran say from inside the house.
"The whole dang town can hear ya."

With all my strength
I give the instruments a good hard kick.

Hattie comes to. "Thank goodness."
Sits up
claps.

A few hundred million miles later
we're floating through space in peace.

CAPTAINS AIN'T AFRAID

I
shut down the engine.

"Have you ever seen anything like it, Hattie?"

"Not in all my born days."

I unbuckle my belt
        decompress the hatch like Buck.
Open the door.
        Check my oxygen levels.
Take off my helmet
        and breathe.

Space air smells sweeter than earth air.
More like them green-apple pies Gran bakes
and wins prizes for.

"Up here
        we can drink from any fountain.
Sit in any seat we want."

Hattie nods, then follows me out.
"When we meet those space people
                don't be scared, you hear?" she says.

I beat my chest. "I'm the captain.
And captains ain't afraid of nothing."

Hattie floats past me
        because there's no gravity in space.

Tiptoeing behind birdcages, we search for stuff
we came with earlier
chicken feet
    tree bark
        rabbit teeth
            eggshells stomped to pieces.

Things we astronauts call by other names
    meteorites
        space dust
            moon rocks.

"Space critters sure are messy," Sister says.
Kneeling
she picks up pine needles
drops 'em into medicine bottles
calls 'em alien bones.

The sound of Gran's bell
    a cooking pot she hits with a wooden spoon
finds us way up here in outer space.
"Suppertime! Y'all come," she says.

We keep exploring
filling our helmets with our finds
lose track of time until I hear something.

    "Squeak."

I
freeze.

Seems like my heart stops too.

Hattie Mae swallows. "It's nothing."

It's *them* and she knows it.

Sister keeps to her space job
collecting marbles
we plan to trade with space pirates
     in case we need to bargain for our lives.

"Squeak."

My fingers find my mouth.
I chew my nails.
Between bites, I ask
     if she heard what I heard.

Sister lies. "No."

"You had to, Hattie. I know it."

I back up
find the darkest part of the roof
the space between the cages and the fence.
Squatting
I squeeze my eyes tight.

"Squeak."
"Squeak."

"James Henry. We know you up there.
You *coward*."

THE BAKER BROTHERS

"Titus Baker, take this."

"Ouch!"

Sister pitches coals over the chicken-wire fence like baseballs.

Her aim is always perfect.
Titus Baker finds that out soon enough.

"Hattie Mae," he shouts up to us.
"Your brother's got it coming, and you know it!"

I try to keep myself calm.
But my mind ignores me
like always.

Run.
Go in the house.
Hide under the kitchen table.

My forehead gets wet as water.
Drips sweat.
I rub my eyes
but cannot wipe my thoughts clean.
So
I take off running.

Pecans fly over the chicken wire like bullets
     hit my chest
      sting my neck
       chase Hattie's birds
rattle the rest still in cages.

I go back to where I was.
Hattie follows.
Crouching low beside me
Sister reminds me that there's a blue moon coming and
when a blue moon shows up
everything
is
set
right
again.

"Everything?"

My hands tremble like collards in a December wind.
"Even me?"
I think of myself the way I used to be.
Brave.

"Even you, James Henry.
Which is why tomorrow you have to start practicing
getting out the house and
used to the world again."

I want to agree
but my thoughts won't go along.
They
ruminate
pester
worry me.

What if she's wrong?
What if I make it to the ocean and drown
once and for all this time?

THE BAKER BROTHERS
PLUS ONE

"James Henry!"

The Baker brothers live
up the road a piece.
Their father's cow always breaks free
finds its way to our house.
The brothers—five of them—are mean as ground hornets.

"Want to go *swimming*?" Titus shouts.
He's the eldest Baker boy.

"Don't let me come down there," says Hattie.

Them Bakers standing with their cousin Red
bring up other things
that scare me
fire
crowds
leaving home
folks touching me
        all except Hattie, Gran, or Daddy.

"Sister,
you won't let 'em get up here, will you?" I ask.

        "No, Brother. I won't."

"Gran won't either, will she?"

        "Never, James Henry."

"And if they come
         they won't find me, right?"

         "They won't get past me, James Henry.
         I'll always protect you. You and me twins."

"But what if there's lots of 'em sometime?
A whole crowd of 'em.
A town's worth
of kids trying to get to me.
Then what?"

         "They know, James Henry, that I
         can whip the whole lot of them, if I must.
         We've been on the moon, haven't we?
         To Ursa Major and back.
         Me and you can do anything."

"Anything."

         "Yeah, twins are like that."

I get on my knees.
Breathe in slow and easy.
Remind myself that long as Hattie is with me,
nothing bad can truly happen.
But then I smell it.

SMOKE.

SISTER SAVES ME, AGAIN

Hattie tells me to stay put
Not to
look.
Not to
think
what she already knows
I'm thinking.

What if the house burns down?
What if Gran can't get out?
What if we're trapped up here?
What help would I be?
     I couldn't even save Ma or Dog.
     Just stood there.
     Not even Hattie knows the whole story.

More smoke floats up to our planet.
I cover my nose and mouth.

Hattie calls for two birds
Wilma
     named after Buck Rogers's assistant
and Pullman
     named for the dignified
     hardworking
     sleeping-car porters
     who formed their very own union.

"Get 'em!" she shouts.

Hattie ain't the captain. I am.
Sometimes she forgets that.

Like now
when she jumps over the chicken-wire fence
leaps to the ground
with her arms wide as dragon wings.

I run to the chicken wire
cheering.

The Bakers and their cousin Red
run too
up the road in every which direction.

Anybody would,
with Hattie and her birds
chasing 'em.

BEDTIME

"Leaves," Hattie said, "that's all it was.
They set a pile on fire."

She stomped 'em out.

But two weeks later
I'm still fretting.

THE DENTIST

Doc Edwards left to wed a gal in Missouri.
Since then
we been short-handed.

There's a new dentist in town, Gran said the other day.
"Now at least we got someone to help folks out
        when the time comes."

But what's a dentist for 'sides pulling teeth?

PART 2

LOSING SISTER

ON OUR WAY TO THE OUTHOUSE

Hattie leads the way
as usual.

I don't let her hold my hand, though I want to.

Down the porch steps we go
slow as honeysuckle blooms in April.

No flashlight, I told her
just in case them Bakers are out here.

We turn left
walking between the house
and a patch of land Gran grows
okra, beans, and cabbages on.

Nellie, our pig, grunts in her pen under a quarter moon.
Jersey, our cow, sleeps standing up,
using her tail to fan the flies away.
The Baker brothers tipped her over once.
Tripped me on my way to school the last time I went.

I stop.

Look in every which direction.

Is that them over there hiding?

I reach back for Hattie's hand.

"It's nothing."

She shuts her eyes.
Follows her feet.
They never forget.

I start and stop again.
"Smoke. You smell it, Hattie?"

She takes my hand.
Her nose roots the air like Nellie's.
"Nope. It was only a few leaves, James Henry.
A pile at the side of the house.
I put that fire out, remember?"

I remember
that we only have a hundred more steps to go.
That
Hattie got school tomorrow
and Gran and me will be all alone again.

"But what if they come when you're at school, Hattie?
What then?"

"You're the captain."

At the darkest part of the road
she turns my hand loose.
Keeps walking.

Not me.
I stop. Stretch my arms wide out
feel the air around me.

"Hattie . . ."

I hear her feet do a quick step
stopping at the bend.

Did she go left, right, straight up?

". . . please . . . come back."

What's that?

    I duck.

Hear something in the bushes
on my right.

    Could be a groundhog
    a muskrat.

I take one step back.

    Or a wobbler
    croak frogs
    feral hogs
    wild dogs
    we got our share.

Other animals come to mind too

    bobcats
    bears
    coyotes.

They'll rip you apart
eat you down to the bone.

My supper fights its way up.
I go down on my knees.

"If I can't see you, James Henry," comes Sister's voice,
"you can't see me.
Then they can't see us."

I look up.
Eyes opened wide.
Blinking.

"What don't you know about this land?" she says.

Blink.
Do it enough and you'll see some things.

"I tell you I made a new friend?
Lottie Jean is her name."

Wipe away them tears, boy. Stand,
I hear my father say.

I get on one foot.
Notice her voice coming from over there.

"She's got Sunday, Monday, Tuesday,
Wednesday, Thursday, Friday,
Saturday dresses.
One for each day."

Hattie only has three.

"No mother to speak of, like us."

"Keep talking, Sister."

She does the opposite.

"Hattie? Hattie?"

I look up.
Recall
that I like the dark
better than daylight.
Notice that my feet
once they get moving
are as good at remembering as hers.

Shaking inside and out
I imagine myself floating in space
stepping over Orion's Belt.

Before I get to the branch
that's been in the bend in the road
all year
I know it's there
like the rusted-out blue Chevy
that met a buck up ahead
and ain't gone nowhere since.

Before I know it
I bump into Sister.
She hugs me.

"I knew you could do it."
She takes me by the shoulders
turns me north. "The lighthouse,
you can see it from here."

I see it miles and miles off
       a white fist in the dark.

"We might as well go tonight," Sister tells me.
"We're practically there anyhow."

I turn around
wishing I had the courage to run back home.

She reaches for my hand.
"I can't stay by your side forever,
James Henry—I'm growing up."

It's the third time she's said that this spring.
Gran is partial to repeating it too.
Maybe it's because of Daddy's last letter.

Ma's cousin Abigail owns a school for girls in Philadelphia.
Says Hattie is always welcome to attend.
Sister and Daddy seem ready to take her up on her offer.
But what about me?

INSIDE THE OUTHOUSE

I close my eyes and
do my business quickly.

OUR HOUSE

Every night before I go to sleep
I look around the house five or six times
to remind myself where things are
just in case the Bakers break in
or Uncle comes after me.

The wood-burning stove and cupboard
are on the right side of the house
the table and chairs sit in the middle
two beds on the left
one for Gran
one for Hattie and me to share
     with a clean bleached sheet long as curtains
separating one bed from the other.

The couch near the window
not far from the front door
is Gran's favorite color
RED, like the kerchief she always wears on her head.

OFF TO SCHOOL

Jewett Road is crowded this time of day
with kids
some barefooted
some not.
    The little ones pitch rocks.
    Girls laugh.
    Boys pull pigtails
    offer to carry the prettiest gals' books.

Most everyone stares on their way past our house.
The mean ones squeak.

The Baker brothers and their cousin
tower over all the rest.
When they step onto the road
a seam splits up the middle.

Titus is tall as a tree,
the color of honey.

He stops outside our house.
With his hands at his mouth
he hollers, "Lottie Jean! Wait up."

Sister stands on the porch steps watching it all.

This Lottie Jean girl don't know any better
I guess
so
she stops.

The others make like a river around a rock.

Titus runs to her.
Folks all except his kin
most times run away from him.

Catching up
he digs his hands deep in his pockets.
Kicks dirt with his bare toes
looks my way
points and squeaks.

Hattie heads down the steps
walks up the road
alone.

THE INSIDE TWIN

I scrape scraps off plates into a slop bucket.
Carry it to the door
leave it for Gran to haul away later for the pig.
Walk to the stove
lift a pot of steaming hot water
dump it into a pan in the sink
wash everything clean
then
help Gran iron other folks' clothes.

In between
I wonder what Hattie's up to.

THE NEW GIRL

Sister calls Lottie Jean nice
polite
proper
a reprieve from us boys
    who mostly live on this road.

"And guess what."

Hattie takes a seat next to me underneath the table,
starts leafing through a Montgomery Ward catalog.

"Her father is the dentist."

MILKING

In a white dress
splattered with yellow daises
Hattie sits wide-legged on a upside-down bucket
squeezing milk from Jersey's udders.

I watch from the kitchen window
like always.

BLAST OFF!

On the roof
I draw circles
on the top end of a wooden hope chest tall as Gran.
Then
saw
two saucer-sized holes in the top end.

Sister hands me a tin of broken mirrors.
Two hours later
we still gluing 'em on the bottom end.

We drag it to the far corner of the roof
stand it
upright
where the moon shines brightest.

Helmets on
we step inside
side by side.

Moonlight shines down
hits the mirrors
lights us up.

Holding hands
eyes closed
we blast off
just when
        the train rolls in.

I'm so happy I could scream.

HATTIE PRETENDING TO BE SOMETHING SHE AIN'T

Them with money
and them without
send their kids to the same
school
the only one for Negroes in these parts.

After the accident
Hattie Mae lost friends
especially them up the road a piece
where folks like the dentist live.

They swore
Sister put on more airs than ever
after Ma met her fate.

So maybe that's why Sister talks lots and lots
about this Lottie Jean.

"A friend, James Henry. Finally,"
she says.

But what she know about her?

POPSICLE TROUBLES

Buck Rogers is having a contest
to find the typical American boy.

The boy with the most Popsicle wrappers
wins.

That's gonna be me!

I have two hundred wrappers already

too many to ever come
from the two Creamsicles
Gran buys us once a month.

That's why I'm thankful for
the white widows up the road.
They have no use for wrappers
given they're old as the sun
so
        once a month on Sundays
they hand them over to Gran
twenty so far.

Gran worries my wrappers is the cause
of the state of their rotten teeth.

I think they just like sweets.

MORE WRAPPERS

Pastor spoke to the church a while back.
Said it would be a good charitable act
if they took it upon themselves
to hand their wrappers over to him
  and him to Gran and Gran to me.

Given what folks say about me
I was surprised.

"The child is touched in the head,"
Pastor's very own wife declared
  the last time she visited.

I was thankful anyhow.
Am still.
I inherited three wrappers her last time here.
Thirty in all.

The other night in a dream
holding tight to my wrappers
I knocked on Buck Rogers's rocket-ship door
and handed 'em over.

"You won," he said
then shook my hand.

Ma clapped.
Gran danced.
Daddy told me how proud he was of me.

A QUESTION FOR SISTER

"Do you ever think about Ma?" I asked Sister.

She asked if I wanted to practice going outside.
I told her I wasn't ready just yet.
She picked up her books and left the house.
I watched her from the window
sitting under Gran's favorite tree
pretending to read.

HATTIE'S NEW TWIN

Sister flies down the porch steps
    runs back up.
Her patent-leather shoes
    tap the wood like raindrops.

"Sorry, James Henry,"
she says
out of breath.

Rushing to the window
she presses her hands to the screen
    touches mine.

We do it every time.
Only today
    she almost forgot.

"Have a good day, James Henry.
Hey, Lottie Jean. Wait up!"
Off Sister goes
tripping on the last step
    falling in the dirt.

By the time Lottie Jean gets to her,
Sister is brushing dirt off her white dress.
    Daddy sent it to her last week.

"Morning, Hattie, James Henry."
Lottie joins in the brushing and fixing up.
Tells Hattie she looks pretty no matter what.
"Don't you think so, James Henry?"

I fiddle with my suspenders.

Her and Sister are long gone when
Titus Baker heads up the road
running.

He don't even have time to
squeak.

If it wasn't for Ma
Titus Baker would be working in the fields right now
instead of headed off to school.

SOMETHING TO THINK ABOUT

Today is practice day, Sister says.
A going-outside-like-the-rest-of-the-world day.
She opens the door
wide.

"No!"
I sit under the table.
Scratch the back of my neck.
Feel more hives coming.

Using Ma's quiet voice, Sister says
"Buck Rogers most likely wants the winning boy
to come where he is
to say hello
stop a spell
introduce himself on the radio."

"I never thought about that,"
I say
eyeing the door.

WHAT UNCLE SAID

In the house
looking out
I ruminate on something Uncle said once.
"You was the same as your Ma
too free
too wild
too concerned with things in the sky
blind to us below who loved you more than anything."

BUCK ROGERS'S FIFTEEN-MINUTE RADIO SHOW

Gran
with a small brush and a pail of water on her lap
sits at the dining table and scrubs her nails clean.

Hattie
across the room on our bed
plucks dead bugs
dry leaves
from Henrietta's and Nutcracker's
feathers and feet.

I'm on the floor on my back
eyes closed
listening
like them
to *Buck Rogers in the 25th Century*
on our brand-new RCA table radio.

A green gas put Buck to sleep for five hundred years.
    That's what you call suspended animation.
Now that he's awake
he travels the universe making it safe for everyone.

From the kitchen table, Gran says
"That man sure have some adventures."

Sister agrees.
"Do you think people live on other planets, Gran?"

"The Lord made more than one. Guess he had his reasons.
Best ask James Henry, though.

He knows more about what's up there than anyone
Negro or white."

That ain't exactly true.
Ma knew a lot.
By the time Daddy gave me my first Buck Rogers comic book
I already knew one day people
would travel, live in space.

The school suspended Ma one whole week
for teaching us things like that.

STAR WALLS

"James Henry," Gran says during a advertisement
break.

"Yes ma'am."

"Time for some new things on these here walls,
don't you think?"

Our wallpaper used to be grasshopper green
till I pasted it over floor to ceiling
with Buck Rogers comic strips
plus maps and pictures ripped from the almanac.

Folks walk up to our house
look in
stop and stare at Saturn and its rings
the Big Dipper
Andromeda
Buck Rogers's friends
articles about what vegetation seeds
need planted when and where
the time of year the moon waxes and wanes
new moons
blue moons
high tides
anything that's got to do with Buck
or what's going on above or planted below.

Busy hands make for a calm brain
Daddy likes to say.
So
he helped me glue things up.
Watched me settle down some.

Encouraged me to paint the ceiling
so I would have a daytime sky over my head
sometimes.

"Gran."

"Yes, boy."

"Maybe we can buy two Popsicles
when we go to market at the month's end."

"Maybe."

"To win the contest
I'll need the most wrappers."

Hattie clears her throat but it's Gran who speaks.
"If anyone can win, you can."

Then she tells us something we never knew.
Ma entered a contest when she was young.
Gran cries some when I ask if she won.

"There was none braver than your mom,"
Gran says like we don't know.

Hattie's birds
agitated
fly around the room
like someone sent in hawks.
She opens the door and frees 'em.

I get back to Ma.
Gran says hush. "He's back on."

HELPING MA WIN

Before Gran tucked us in last night
she finished that story she started about Ma.

The contest winner got a bag of peppermint candy sticks
for beating all the other runners
up the lighthouse steps.

Ma's heart was set on winning, Gran said.
But the lighthouse keeper put a stop to that
turned her away at the starting line.

"Your leg," he said.

Ma cried and cried, Gran said.
I knew why.

When Ma was born, her legs didn't match.
One was longer.
     One shorter.
She rocked when she walked.
But so what?
Ma could've won that race even with her legs.
They never stopped her from being a teacher
or the best mom and daughter ever.

Last night in a dream
me and Ma ran up those lighthouse steps
     all ninety-six.

She won!

UP A TREE WITH MA

Teaching class
outside
with us kids sitting in trees
was Ma's favorite thing.

Always below
on the ground
looking up
she smiled while she taught us
to figure numbers
spell words long as fingers
learn about countries where everybody was free.

Even the Baker boys didn't complain back then
but the grown-ups did.

They called Ma odd. Citified.

Ma would smile
laugh
and say
"And you have a good day yourself."

Once in church
Titus Baker asked Ma a question about gravity.
She had to answer, right?
But she didn't have the right to drop
the church program on the floor, Uncle told her.
The women rolled their eyes.
Titus Baker got his answer.
Gravity holds everything down

including the program
the church building and everybody in it,
      Ma told him.

"I understand now," he said, dropping the Bible.
Ma caught it before it hit the floor.
But
not too many people spoke to her afterward.

SCHOOL'S OUT

Finally
school is over for the summer.
I'll have Sister all to myself,
I thought.
But soon as her chores were done
she ran up the road
to spend the day with Lottie.

A LETTER TO DADDY

Today
I wrote a letter
put sand in the envelope
told Daddy it was stardust.
That's what Ma called it.

She knew better.
I know better than to write her a letter too
but I do.

A VISITOR IN THE HOUSE

With pink satin rag ties on her plaits
Lottie Jean
marches into our house
nose stuck up.

"Well, hello, James Henry."

Who asked her in?
Nobody.

She took the steps up to the house
tapped on the front door twice
walked in uninvited.

No wonder Gran looks surprised.

Lottie Jean clears her throat.
Repeats herself. Adding Gran this time.
"Hello, James Henry. Morning, Mrs. Walker."

I stay where I am
parked under the table
peeking out.

Head high
shoulders back
like there's a crown on her head
she walks past the couch
then the table and our beds
right into Gran's kitchen area
not once asking permission.

Lottie Jean moves different from Hattie Mae.

She takes small steps
like some take small bites
holds her books close
blinks
too much for my pleasure.

With her hand on her hip
Gran stirs oats in a pot on the stove.
"Morning, child. Hattie gone be in
soon as she's done with her birds."

"James Henry." Lottie Jean turns full around
heads my way till Gran advises her to stop.

I do not like people in the house
Gran explains. Except her and Hattie.

"Oh," Lottie says.

Hattie didn't tell her everything, I see.

Lottie Jean rocks on her heels.
Fixes her eyes on my ceiling sky.

"Can I talk to him?
I'd like to ask him a question."

She points up.
"Are there really three hundred and sixty-five stars
up there like Hattie says?"

"Gran!"

"Yes, baby."

"Make her leave."

"Now, James Henry . . ."

"I'm feeling poorly."

"But Hattie's got a right to friends."

She'll tell everyone
what she saw.
Me.
A mouse on the floor.
A coward.

"Gran! Please."

I sit up
hold my knees
rock myself
remind myself not to fret.

Nothing works.

"Gran!"

She stirs the pot
my insides stir
my stomach churns
until I'm 'bout doubled over.
"Aaaah."

She'll tell . . . I know it.
Uncle told Pastor, didn't he?
Cousin told Teacher

something's
wrong
with
the
boy.
"He knows more about that night than he lets on."

"Please, Gran."

Sixty-one
with spider-long legs and arms
Gran ushers Lottie Jean to the door.

"Go, child.
Next time wait outside."

My heart eases some.
Gran goes back to her cooking
humming
like the day never had a hiccup.

MAD HATTIE

Normally Sister hugs me goodbye
before leaving the house
kisses my cheek.

Nothing today. Not even a salute.

Sister walks over to our bed
sits
kicks
off her work boots
slips
into her patent-leather shoes.
Eyes me.

Even my X-ray vision can't find
a smile.

Hattie grabs her lunch pail off the table,
books for playing school.
Shoos Nutcracker and Pickle away
leaves.

I race to the window and watch her follow Lottie Jean
like mosquitoes after sweaty skin.
Why
when she's got me?

HATTIE'S RIGHTS

"Hattie's got a right to be mad," Gran says.
"She likes that child."

I know.

"Has a right to friends."

I know.

"You too."

I got Hattie Mae.

PART 3

INVADERS

ALIENS

Gran's friends will be here any minute.
No matter how many times she'll tell 'em
not to peek through
the window at the boy
like a bear in a zoo
            they're gonna.
Which is why Hattie says I need an antidote
        medicine
        a remedy
        something to ease my mind
        to free my insides
        so folks won't seem so bothersome to me.

Her answer is the blue moon.
On *Buck Rogers*
antidotes come in test tubes.

Ma's antidote was education.
Because no matter how you spoke or looked
where you lived
what you had or didn't have
getting an education and learning was your
birthright
as much as breathing air, she said.

IGNORE THEM

At the sink
pumping water till it runs clear
I fill test tubes one by one
soak my hands
     splash my shirt.

The women walk up the porch steps
one behind the other like soldiers.

In dresses past their knees
they stare straight ahead.

Toting
     purses
     filled with sewing and knitting needles
wearing wide-brim straw hats with bird feathers stitched to 'em
     they look stiff and dignified.

Breathe
I tell myself.
Do like Gran says and ignore 'em.

PASTOR'S WIFE

"Where's James Henry?"

The pastor's wife makes her way to the window.
"For once he's not under the table, I see."

My palm starts itching.

She yells my name.
"James Henry! I see you in there."

I ignore her.
Head for the pantry
open the door wide
disappear behind it.

Floor to ceiling the pantry is filled
with Gran's cooking things.
    Flour
    a five-cent brown bag of sugar nearly empty
    peaches, peas, string beans, and apples canned by
    Gran and us
    a bag of bicarbonate of soda
Gran's cure for what ails ya.

"I only wish to be sociable, James," the pastor's wife insists.

I take a pinch of soda
drop it in a test tube
watch the concoction foam up
bubble over
run down my fingers like lava.

Finally
it's ready.

I lift it high
       drink till it empties.
Repeat.

Walking backward
so as not to catch the pastor's wife's eyes
I make my way to my laboratory.

She pesters me
always.

"I can see you, you know."
I turn
look past her at Gran
who explains
but seems tired of explaining
that I am not like other children.

Wish I was.

"I have a wrapper for you."
Pastor's wife waves the wrapper like a flag.
Still
I do not surrender.
I look at Gran
who said she's beholden to these women
       when pigs need slaughtering
       or the cow goes too far off.

It's their sons and husbands
       that step in since Daddy's gone

and Uncle can't.

BROKEN THINGS

They sit in a circle rocking
threading needles
stitching squares to make a wedding quilt
     for Pastor's seventh daughter
gabbing about the new dentist
when they ain't talking about me, that is.

"Of course the Baker boys torment him.
Sticks always get thrown at the dim-witted and odd,"
the pastor's wife says.

The other ladies raise their voices
ask how she can be so uncharitable toward me.

Gran rocks.

I settle myself under the table
put on a space helmet with antennas
to block out the sound.

For the next hour
I fiddle with wires
pliers
a socket and a battery
I mean
to mount to our rocket ship
for a new source of energy and light.

I ignore them
till Mrs. Sable brings up Daddy and me.

"Do you think he's ashamed of James Henry?"

I never thought that.

Gran says there's no truth to it.

But what if he is?

Daddy used to write to us every night.
Then the letters came
once a week
now twice a month.

What if he's ashamed of me, mad?
Uncle is.

The pastor's wife leans left
spits chew in Gran's tobacco can
says I am the reason for all their troubles.

Gran's shoulders rise
like crab claws are pinching her.
She tries to defend me but can't.

I crawl from under the table
face the window facing them
swing my pitching arm
stop myself for Gran's sake.
Turning right
I find the mirror
on the wall
near the sink
and send them pliers flying.

Glass comes at me like bees
stings

bites
cuts my arms and chin
nicks my shoulder
makes me bleed.

Gran beats her friends into the house.

LIONS

"I told you, Martha. Day by day he's worse,"
the pastor's wife says.

In the kitchen
Gran rips rags into pieces
needed to clean my wounds
dress my cuts.

"He's a peaceable boy," she says.
"Never done this kind of thing before."

One lady sweeps up glass.
Another helps Gran with the rags.

Pastor's wife brings up Uncle
who told her husband
maybe it was time for me
to go to that school for kids
too intolerable
to live at home anymore.

Gran looks sad.

I smack my head all over.

Stupid. Stupid. Stupid.

Miss Priestly comes to me
with her hands raised like I might rob her.

"James Henry has been through a lot," she says.
"Who would expect him to be well so soon?"

She used to be a teacher in South Carolina.
Now she's old.

With a butter-soft voice
she explains everything before she does it.
"There's glass on your clothes," she says
while Gran wipes away blood.
"I'll take care of the rest.
Is that okay?" she asks.

I back into the table.

Gran tells her what everyone should know.
"He don't like to be touched."

Miss Priestly understands.
Pastor's wife don't.
She takes me by the wrist.
Says it's time
Gran and Pastor stopped coddling me.

They'll lock me up
put me away.

I shove her good and hard.
Nearly knock her off her feet.

Them women circle me like lions.

BACK TO THE LABORATORY

Gran steps in.
Shoves Miss Priestly.
Elbows the pastor's wife.

"Get away from him!
And get out of my house.
Hattie and I can do what needs done round here
      good as any man can."

The rag in her hand is flecked with red
when she says,
"Them that ain't
gone in the next minute
will wish they was."

They scurry out the house like mice.
All but the pastor's wife.

I go back to my laboratory under the table,
shaking like a horse being bitten by flies.

AN APOLOGY

Pastor's wife bends low
looks me in the eyes
like she sees me for the first
time ever.

Slow and easy she apologizes.
She is known to be contrary, she says.
"Pastor himself admits to that.
Much as he prays for me he laments
that getting me into heaven
will be easy as shoving a horse through a keyhole."

Even I laugh at that.

Dressed in white
the pastor's wife sits on the floor like it's no big deal.

"You twins had a hard year
with your mother nearly drowning."

She looks up at Gran
offers to take me to the dentist to get my arm stitched.
"But I know he's not ready to leave the house yet."

Bad things will happen if I do.

She pats my hand.
Stands.
Rushes out the door.

DOCTOR DENTIST

The pastor's wife rode her wagon up the road a spell
and brought the dentist here for fear
I would bleed to death
at least that's what she tells me.

Along the way she picked up Hattie Mae.

"I've never seen the boy act up with her around,"
Pastor's wife tells Gran.

LOTTIE'S FATHER

Dr. Cummings is a short pudgy man
with jet-black wavy hair
and front teeth long as fangs
    pearly white.

He leans in close
examines the tourniquet Gran put on my arm.

In bed
I kick the quilt off
punch the air
scream my throat raw.
"Hattie! Help me, Hattie!"

Her birds take off flying.
The dentist stumbles back.

Gran blocks Hattie
who is standing next to her
then turns to the dentist.
"Some say he's peculiar.
Well, he ain't. He's got a condition, that's all."

She sits herself down on the right side of the bed.
Wipes sweat from my forehead, cheeks, and chin.
Presses her palm to my belly and chest
till my breathing regulates itself.

Dr. Cummings scratches his temple. Pulls at his hair.
Asks everyone to leave the room
    including Hattie.

Pastor's wife starts the parade.

Sister crosses her arms
stands guard at the foot of our bed
eyeing the dentist.
"He needs me, Doctor," Hattie says.

I do.

"He won't cry or anything as long as I'm here.
Right, Captain?"

"Right." I look at the dentist.

Hattie sits on the bed beside me.
"Doctor?" It's Gran.

His warm eyes turn to Sister.
"I could use an assistant."

Hattie jumps up and down
talks a mile a minute.
Tells him she is used to assisting me on flights.

He doesn't seem surprised.

NO ESCAPE

Sister races across the room
onto the roof
returns with our space helmets.
The ones that protect your brains
from radio waves.

"If he doesn't have this on, it'll go
mighty hard for you, Dr. Cummings."

She puts hers on first.
Excuses herself
steps in between Gran, Dr. Cummings, and me.
Righting the helmet on my head
she reminds me that she'd never
let a thing happen to me, ever.

      Ma said those words in the ocean.

The dentist looks at Gran
sticks his hand in a black bag.

Under the covers I go.
To the other end of the bed
with Hattie's birds flying
screeching overhead.

When I come up for air
there he is
standing over me smiling.

Back I go.
Crawling fast as ants on hot sand.

Doc meets me again.

Breathing hard
I stay put this time.

WHAT PEOPLE DON'T KNOW
ABOUT ME

With my head outside the sheets
my good hand holding tight to the edge
I keep an eye on his black bag.

He'll cut you to pieces.

Out comes thread and needles for sewing skin
plus
     peroxide
     iodine
     and a bottle of pills to settle me.
     All that's necessary to put me back together, he says.

Like Hattie put her rag doll together
but never got all the cotton back inside?

Gran takes Dr. Cummings by the arm
leads him across the room.
Tells him about Ma and how I nearly drowned too.

I wish my father was here.

SOMETHING IN COMMON

The dentist says
when bad things happen to us
we can go deep inside ourselves and hide
but if folks give me time
I'll find my way back to myself.

It's a surprise to me when I nod.
A surprise when his eyes find the ceiling and he smiles.

Sister tells him how long it took me to draw
and paint the sky
blue with stars and two daytime suns and a moon besides.
And why I should win the Buck Rogers Typical American Boy
Contest.

That's how I learn *Buck Rogers* is Dr. Cummings's
favorite radio show
just like it is mine.

ALMOST LIKE ME

I sit up
lean on my elbows when he tells me
he's never missed an episode.

Me either.

Three times a week
for fifteen minutes
Monday through Wednesday
it's on.

"James Henry has more Popsicle wrappers
than any boy in this neighborhood, I'm sure."
Sister sticks her hand out.
"If you have some, we'll take 'em. Thank you very much."

Five more steps and Doc
is standing over me and taking off the tourniquet.

"Fudgesicles are my favorite Popsicle. And you?"

I pull my arm but can't pull free.

He digs in his doctor's bag.
Promises to give his wrappers to me
if I'm a big boy through all this.

I try not to throw up.

"Close your eyes, James Henry." It's Hattie.
"Climb in the spaceship. Ride to the moon with me."

I blink.
Rub my eyes too many times to count.
Not that it helps.
They're heavy as wet logs
after the dentist slides the needle in
and the medicine gets to work.

"What if I wake up with too many arms?" I hear myself say.

They laugh.

HAPPY

Buck Rogers is on the radio
I'm on my belly spread-eagle on the floor
surrounded
by Hattie
Gran,
and my two hundred wrappers
plus twenty-six extras from the dentist.

HAPPY.

After the show
I take my time licking my Popsicle.
Sister finishes hers lickety-split.

Gran says a prayer for Ma.
Us too.
Then we three dance to a song Gran sings.

FOR MY FATHER

Gran's friend's words won't turn me loose.
So
I wrote Daddy again.
Are you sorry I'm your son?

I'm hoping for an answer soon.

COWS AND CHICKEN COOPS

Across from the kitchen window
on a stool outside the barn
Sister sits wiping Jersey's udders clean
    to keep germs out the milk.

I remind her that we're headed to Jupiter tonight.

"Can't, Captain." Hattie turns and faces me.
"Lottie Jean's stopping by.
Don't worry.
She won't step foot in the house."

It's been a month since school let out.
And this Lottie Jean is still around.

WATCHING

Moo.

Hattie pulls on them udders
up
down
up
down
like ropes at church that swing bells
that tell everyone when to
come in
or what time of day it is.

In green rubber boots
and a sunburst dress past her knees
she squirts milk into the pail
into the air at flies that pester her.

I miss that.

Hattie looks over her shoulder at me.
"Now stop it, James Henry."

"Stop what, Hattie?"

"Fretting."

She quits milking.
Stands.
Picks up the pail by the handle.
Sits it on the floor close by the barn door.
Walks up to the chicken coop at the far end of the barn
past a rusted-out tractor

rakes hanging on the wall
bales of hay on the floor.

Hattie sings.
The chickens too.
She leaves the barn with
the milk pail in one hand
a basket of eggs in the other.

Inside the house I empty her hands
walk over to the kitchen
put things in their place.

Hattie takes my place under the table.
I join her when I can.
Tell her about the letter I wrote to Daddy.
The words Mrs. Sable said
the day I broke the mirror.

"Nothing new, James Henry.
It's been said one way or the other
by nearly everybody in town, right?"

She's right. Always right.

LAUNDRY DAY

They pull up one behind the other
Gran's regulars.

"Morning, Auntie," Mrs. Mary says.

Gran doesn't like being called that.
But white people won't use *Miss* or *Mrs.*
for women like Ma, Gran, and their friends.
Nonetheless
she says, "Morning," and smiles.

Mrs. Mary's son lifts a full basket
out the car
     lugs it to the side of the house.

The next car pulls up behind the first.

"Morning, Auntie."

Gran nods.

Marshall Bell hops out the car before his mother stops.

She beeps the horn
wags her finger
smiles Gran's way
reminds her to put in extra starch.

From the kitchen window
I see Sister and three laundry tubs
that Gran's mother handed down to her

one for washing
one for rinsing
the third for bluing clothes white.

Sister in her yellow dress
rushes to the bushes
snaps off branches
sits awhile
strips 'em clean.
Broken branches
added to newspaper
go under the middle tub
right before Hattie sets the fire.

After the water boils
in the clothes go.

Gran and Hattie will
hang 'em on the line later.
Gran and me will do the ironing.
Pastor's middle son Jerome
will carry 'em in his wagon to them that's paying.

He gets the tip I used to get.

A BAD WIND

Hattie Mae and me
    stake our claim on Jupiter
stick a tall
thin pole in a Crisco can
six inches deep with dirt.

She made the flag
from Daddy's old plaid shirt
said, "Shhh, who'll know unless we tell?"

Lucky us
a wind kicks up
blowing hard enough for the flag to salute.

But sure enough
that wind blows other things our way.

Lottie Jean.

KEEPING SISTER HAPPY

Sister takes off running
stops at the fence
looks over
nearly tips over
so happy you'd think Daddy had come home.

With one hand on the fence
she turns my way
smiles.
"It's Lottie Jean, James Henry."
Like I can't recognize her voice.

She lied.
Said Lottie Jean wasn't coming after all.
That me and her could do whatever I wanted.

"Can she come up?
I told her about our adventures."

No
No
No
No

"Well, can she?"

I'm the captain. I make the rules.
But Sister is set on having a friend
this one in particular.

I am set on keeping my sister
so
I say yes.

"But tell her not to talk to me."

CAPTAIN LOTTIE

Keep an eye on a girl like Lottie Jean.
She's got ways and ideas
that Sister seems taken with.

Instead of letting Lottie Jean sit on the stool
Sister gives her a seat in our rocket ship
the captain's chair.

I stay behind the birdcages
watching.

Lottie Jean steers the wheel.
Points to the sky.
Asks Hattie if she wants one of her dresses
a pink one with white polka dots.
"I've outgrown it."

Sister nods.
Smiles.
Puts up five fingers
says this will be her fifth dress.
The most ever.
Ma did not like to spend money on such.

Lottie Jean says she may have more to pass on.

Why?
She hardly knows Sister.

Soon they leave the sky behind
talk about boys
the Bakers plus a boy who sits by Sister at church.
Martin.

Who?

I don't know him since
I ain't been to church in a month of Sundays.

Lottie Jean covers her lips and snickers.
"Red Baker likes you, I think."

He's the Bakers' red headed
out-of-town cousin
who came to visit last year,
never left.

Lottie Jean
insists
that those Bakers aren't all bad.

Sister and me know better.

Only for some reason
she doesn't say so.
She fingers Lottie Jean's white lace collar
and smiles.

Not long after
she excuses herself.

Stepping out the rocket ship
Sister passes a basket full of things
astronauts need in space
helmets
test tubes for experiments
tinfoil
and such.

When Hattie gets close to me,
she stops—
"Be nice, James Henry"—
then she disappears inside.

Lottie Jean climbs out the rocket ship.

BAD-LUCK LOTTIE

Run.

For once
I ignore myself
    walk to the front of the cages instead
set Nutcracker, Pullman, and
Sarasota free.

Two of them land on her shoulders.

Traitors.

Lottie Jean smiles my way.
"Do you like my hair, James Henry?"

I blink.

"Daddy found a hairdresser to do it once a week."

Why's a girl need to bat her eyes so much?

One step
two steps later
Lottie Jean is so close
    I can smell her breath.

I step back.
Close my eyes.
Feel my toes burning.

"Truly, James Henry, I do not bite."

My legs buckle.

When she tells me she's no different than me
I open one eye.

"I'm bad luck."

Inside myself I offer my condolences.

"So you do not have to be afraid of me. We're the same.
You and me."

No one's ever said that about me except Ma and Sister.

"I was born on Friday the thirteenth."

That's not so bad.

"A hour later our house burned down."

I step back.

"Bad luck follows me like a black cat."
Hattie's birds head for their cages.

It's her bad luck
that brought her and the dentist to Seed County, Lottie tells me.
"We came home one day and there it was
every stick of our furniture out on the curb."

How was that her fault?

"And which day did it happen?
On my birthday."

Lottie Jean smiles.
"But I do not let trouble make me uncheerful.
I'll outrun it one day
I'm sure I will."

She doesn't say a word for a while.
Then out it comes
something Sister never should have shared.

"Hattie Mae told me about the blue moon."

I shake my head no.

"But, James Henry, I just have to go!"

I got my own troubles. More than I can count.
Hattie and me would be fools to court more of it.

But Lottie Jean is like Sister.
She wants what she wants when she wants it.

"Won't you think about it?" she says,
batting her eyes at the moon.
"It's a lot of weight to carry, being so unlucky."

DOING THINGS MY WAY

The lightkeeper always said Ma was good company
that I was too
when she'd bring me along.

But Ma had to work late that night.
She told me to go home.

I knew I wouldn't.

I walked a mile with Dog
who lived wherever he pleased
and always joined me and Ma along the way.

We named him.

LOTTIE JEAN AGAIN

Under the table
my back facing her
I empty one test tube into another.

"James Henry!"

I ignore Lottie Jean
    like last week never happened.

She keeps talking anyhow.
Brings up her father.
He took my stitches out a while ago.
Sent more wrappers today.

Thanks
I say in my head.

Lottie Jean offers
to mail 'em to Buck Rogers for me.

I'm not ready yet.

Sister asks if I'm ready to practice going outside.

"No."

That blue moon is coming, she says.
Due in less than a month.

"I know."

She looks tired.
But not too tired to invite Lottie Jean
to sip lemonade outside under the tree
Gran planted in honor of Ma.

ME, SISTER, AND THE SUN

Gran didn't know till I told her
stars shine in the daytime too.
You can't see 'em because the sun is so bright
closer to earth than any other star, besides.
The brightest star in our solar system.

Lottie Jean is the sun.
When she's around
Sister doesn't notice me.
I'm still shining, though.

POOR HOME TRAINING

The Baker brothers came by throwing rocks.
Hattie Mae threw 'em right back
jumped the fence and chased 'em off
    till I couldn't see her nor her birds.

She was gone a mighty long while this time.

When she got back
she had Lottie Jean on her mind.

"Lottie thinks if we talk to them Bakers
maybe we could change their temperament."
    Sister takes a seat in the rocket ship.
"But no."
Her fists ball up.
"They were raised poorly, and it shows.
Even Ma couldn't help 'em, remember?" she says.

I remember Ma saying she would never quit on them.
Never give up on anyone when it came to learning.
Inside the house
I write a letter to Ma, hoping Sister will add some words to it.

No.
Hattie Mae says, "Not this time."

She always says that.

ENOUGH

I think Sister has had enough of me.

COUNTDOWN

Hattie quits singing.
Her rope
and
feet
slow
down some too.

"One," she says. "Two."

I yell out the window.
"I'm not ready just yet, Hattie Mae."

I mistakenly told Sister that today could be a practice day.
A coming-outside-for-a-little-while-during-the-day day.
I was wrong.
I don't have it in me.
But Hattie Mae holds a body to their promises.

I tuck myself tight between the folds of the curtains
wishing I was invisible
had powers that could make me disappear.

"Two and a half," Lottie Jean says from the steps.

"You got no part of this, Lottie Jean!
And, Sister, you are not the boss of me!"

Sister's rope dangles from her fingers.
Coils
        on
the ground
        like a snake
once she drops it.

With her eyes on me
she lifts her hand high
puts up three fingers.

I'd run
if I weren't scared
she'd catch me
before my feet
found the floor.

"Four and a half."

"I'm feeling poorly, Hattie Mae, and you know it!"

"Five."
Sister starts walking toward the house.
Gran keeps rocking.
Lottie Jean doesn't say a word.

HOLDING ME TO MY PROMISE

Steps creak underneath Sister's flat feet.

The floor
under my feet
creaks too
when I jump up and down
begging Gran to make Sister leave me be.

Hattie is determined
to hold me to my word.

She works the doorknob.

Turning
twisting it
this way and that
Sister yells
"Open up, you ornery thing!"

She beats and bangs
on it
like it has to do what she says
like I got to do what she says

when both me and the door
are stuck.

Don't she understand?
I want to go swimming—like any kid.

Want to go to school
run up the road past Connors' Mills

take the hill to Mr. Handlin's smelly old barn
sneak a ride on his pig.

I miss skipping rocks in Thompson's pond
playing ball with sticks
sitting sky-high up in me and Hattie's favorite tree.

Most of all I miss
Ma being home in the kitchen
making breakfast
teaching in the schoolhouse laughing all the time
Daddy walking down the road whistling his way home to us.

Hattie ought to understand.
Gran does.

"Let him be, child."
Gran puts her knitting in a basket at her side.
"When your father comes home—"

Hattie Mae gives the door one last punch.
"That's not for months!" she yells.

Gran slides her wrinkled hand into her apron pocket.
"He sent a letter. For you, James Henry.
But you gots to come get it."

Daddy answered my letter?

"Have Hattie bring it to me."

She could, Gran says. But since I'm the captain
the one in charge
she figures I should come get my own letter

stamped and addressed to me by my very own father
who went north
to make money so Ma could be taken care of properly.

"Hand it to Hattie.
She'll hand it to me,"
I tell Gran through the window.

Hattie Mae folds her arms tight.

"Then you bring it to me, Gran.
Once ya done rocking."

She grumbles about being too old to raise young'uns.
"Well, back to the postman it goes," I hear her say.

I ask Sister again
and again
and again
because I know she'll do it.
She'll do anything for me.

But not this time.
"Suit yourself, James Henry,"
she says, taking a seat on the steps
next to Lottie Jean.

DETROIT

It takes a good long while for Hattie to come inside.
Joining me, she hands over the letter.

Daddy talks about Detroit some.
How he started out working for Ford
on the foundry floor
now he's a mechanic.

All day long. That's what I do, boy.
Lift
rivet
sweat for you, Ma, and Hattie Mae.
You know I love y'all to the moon and back, right?

I know, Daddy.

Sister and me laugh at the words he says he learned from a
    friend up there.

Off the cob.
Moo juice.
Swap pop.

The way he says
    they dance nothing like us down here.

I close my eyes
watch him and Ma dancing across the living room floor
    like they did every Saturday night
with Count Basie's band playing on the radio.

"Who loves ya?" he'd say to her.

"You."
She'd lay her head on his shoulder.

"From the first time I seen you . . ."
Daddy always got choked up.

She'd finish his words.
"I loved you."

"What's a smart woman like you
want with a sow's ear like me
who never made it past the eighth grade?"
Sister says, repeating Daddy.

I give the answer Ma always gave.

"You may not know which astronomer
calculated the circumference of the earth,
but you are one of the most intelligent people I know."

"I know."
He'd stand taller.
"The handsomest man in the world too."

They'd start dancing again.
Laughing.
Kissing.
Holding one another tight.

Sister and I hug each other too
smiling.

YOU CAN BE SURE OF IT

I get back to Daddy's letter.

Your mother misses you.
    I'm sure of it.
And she don't blame you one bit.
    I'm sure of it.

Neither do I.

She would say it's not your fault.
That ain't no one is to blame
not you
not her nor Dog.

Things happen.
That's all.

Families
love each other in good weather and bad,
your mother said that time I lost my job after I lost my temper
again after you got ahold of acid and burned a hole in Gran's
        best dress.
Remember?

I remember.

Good weather or bad
I'm still your Dad.
She's still Ma.
Loving you and Hattie Mae more than our own selves.
Y'all can be sure of it.

IN HIS SHOES

Hattie smiles.
Me too.
"Don't you feel better, James Henry?
I do."

"There's more to read,"
I say.
"Just a little."

"Go on.
I haven't seen you look this happy in a long time."

We read together in our heads.

James Henry,
when it seems you too scared to stand on your own two feet
stand in my shoes

the ones you polished last
the ones sitting under Gran's bed.

In a flash
I run across the room
walk up to Gran's bed
kneel
feel around until I find his Sunday-only shoes.

I seat myself cross-legged on the floor
with his shoes close beside me
and read on.

How will you get to the sky
if you don't get out the front door?

Yeah, how?

One day, he goes on to say,
I will fill his shoes
do more than he's ever done.
But I have to get out first
fly
like Hattie's birds.
The way him and Ma taught us.

Black and shiny
my father's shoes
don't complain
when I squeeze them to my chest
then
sit them on the floor
stand over them like a statue.

I step my feet inside
one at a time
slip
slide
across the floor
over to the door
opening it slow and easy
peeking out.

"Hattie."

"Yes, Brother."

"I didn't ask for this condition."

My father's shoes lead me onto the porch.

Sister, close behind, says, "Of course you didn't, James Henry."

Daddy's shoes
are like his feet
giant.
I feel giant-sized too.

Marching
with my arms rising and falling
like hammers
I make my way over to Gran
who hugs me so hard I can't breathe.

Hattie takes my right hand.
Gran the left.
Inside my father's shoes my toes wiggle.
And for a little while
I'm not afraid of anything.

A WHOLE NEW WORLD

The sun's so bright it hurts my eyes.
Not that I shut 'em.
I keep looking
watching
hoping the day won't run away from me.

STILL HERE

"What's that?" I ask.

"Gran's roses. Sweet as honey.
How'd you forget?" Sister asks.

"Bigger than ever." Gran steps in.
"Most likely
showing off 'cause you out here."

Lottie Jean waves from the garden.
Fills her skirt full of figs from a tree
PopPop planted
    the night he married Gran.

I ignore her.
But not the pecan tree near the barn.
I miss picking 'em.
Smashing 'em.
Hitting Sister in back the head with 'em.

"James Henry?"

"Hush," I tell Sister.

She listens to me for once.
I
listen
to the wind
to the cow mooing
the lumber mill sawing a ways off.

Everything moves and talks.

Nothing's in a hurry at all
not Gran back in her rocker
not the truck climbing a highway close by
nor Lottie Jean chewing on figs
spitting out seeds.

NEWS ABOUT MA

Gran pulls out her own letter.
Written to her by Daddy.
Everything he says is about Ma.

Outdoors excited me so
    I nearly forgot about her.
Whispering to Hattie
I ask if that was wrong.

"Once in a while, James Henry,
it's okay to have fun. To enjoy yourself a bit.
Ma wouldn't hold nothing like that against you."

Gran nods.
Reads the letter out loud.

Ma is getting better, Daddy says.
Learning to walk again.
To talk again.
Getting good care up there
from him, Daddy's kin, and old friends.

Twenty-four hours a day they watch over her
talk to her
pray
work her limbs
wash her clean.

Besides the ocean water
it was the jellyfish that sealed her fate.
Soon as he could Daddy took her north.

Gran starts rocking
praying
thanking God.

Lottie Jean walks up to us.
Takes our hands.
Holds on tight.

I don't say a thing.

HATTIE'S WAY

Since I'm outside
Sister thinks I should stay out
head up the road
fish in the pond
hitch a ride out of here
no stopping till we're at the place
where my troubles began.

I back up.
Back up some more
till the screen door scrapes
the heels of Daddy's shoes.

Gran pardons herself.
Opens the door, heads inside.
Nutcracker and Pullman sneak out.

"Time to go, James Henry. That moon is just a day away."
Hattie leans down
dusts off her jet-black patent-leather Mary Jane shoes
        bought at Parsons by Gran.

Of course, Sister couldn't try 'em on in the store.
"I never wanted to in the first place," she told the owner.
Then she marched herself out the front door
with her nose high as heaven and me close behind.
Gran too. Proud.

A STORM ON THE WAY

I look down at Daddy's shoes
whisper to Sister that even if I wanted to
I couldn't go nowhere in these.

In a flash
Sister and Lottie Jean go inside hunting
for shoes, they say.

Not long after, I notice it
a car kicking up dust along Pickle Patch Highway.
Uncle.

FIRE

His pea-green Studebaker rolls off the highway
never bothering to stop
at the stop sign
put up by the county to stop folks from flying
through our part of town.

I say the first words that come to mind.

"Fire! Fire! Fire!"

Sister rushes out carrying my shoes.
Lottie Jean asks what's burning round here.

"There's the fire," Gran says
pointing Uncle's way.

UNCLE'S OTHER TWIN

Uncle found me
breathed life back into me.

Before then
he was my favorite uncle.
I was his godson.
The sun.
More like him than his own twin
    he'd say.

Now
I'm his enemy.

FREE

A heap of dust follows Uncle's wheels.

"Come, James Henry, please."
Sister holds her hand out.
"We'll leave now.
Figure things out along the way."

Gran asks what all the whispering's about.
I step out of Daddy's shoes.

Uncle's car gets stopped at the railroad track
after the arm comes down
and the lights flash a warning.

He sticks his head out the window
lifts his brown hat
waves it.

Gran walks over to the door.
Holds it open wide
says for me to get inside. "Now."

Two more of Hattie's birds fly out.

OUT OF TIME

The train whistles
rumbles on its way by
shakes
the ground
our house too.

Uncle's car rolls over the tracks
    bumpety
    bumpety
    bump
slows to a stop in front the house.

And just like that
I'm freezing cold
shaking
the way he found me.

THINGS THAT USED TO BE

He steps out the car
waves
at the train with a smile on his face.

Then turns my way.

I see it in his eyes
a wanting for things long gone
his porter uniform maybe.
His old job back working on the train.
Three of his fingers.

All lost because of me.

FACE TO FACE

Uncle walks onto the porch
gives Gran a kiss to the cheek.

Ignores me.

"Morning, Hattie Mae."
He hugs Sister like always.

She don't like it much
now that he don't like me much.

He sits in a rocker
hat in hand.
"Who's your friend?" he asks
but doesn't wait for the answer.

Lottie Jean makes her way over to him.
Goes on and on.
"How are you this fine day?"
"Have you met my father? He's a dentist."
"How come James Henry doesn't talk to anyone?"

Uncle ignores her
but not me this time.

"Must be a storm brewing
the world ending
if you're out here, boy."

Gran slaps her hands together.
"Get! I mean it. Go!"
She points to Uncle.

"Right now, son. If you can't visit
without tormenting him so."

Uncle apologies
        to her.

Gran collects herself.
Opens the door.
Promises to rustle up coffee
black as midnight
fresh biscuits smothered in warm
brown gravy
crackling.
Uncle's favorites.
He stays put.
Me too.

"Y'all both stuck."
Gran looks sad for the first time in a long while.
"Time to let the past go. Aberdeen would want that."

A WAY OUT

I was never stuck, Sister told me once.
"Like the Pole Star isn't stuck in one spot
    though people think it is."

The Pole Star
is the North Star
is Polaris
one thing with three names.
    A way out if you take it.

I have three names too.
Coward.
James Henry.
The boy who almost got his mother drowned.
But there's a way out if I take it, Sister whispers.

I back up some.
Take another step
then another
and another
one two three or so
till I'm down the porch steps
with nothing but thick warm brown
North Carolina dirt holding me up.

GOING

Run
fast as you can

FIGHTING MAD

I
pass the pigpen
the outhouse
the deer hit by the car
    the parts of him that ain't ate up anyhow.

I bend
when the road does
    lift my knees higher
        pump my arms faster
            ball my fingers tighter.
Try not to cry.
Not to stop.
Not to think about all the bad things
    that can happen when you leave the house.

I stop
when I see what's ahead of me.

Tree limbs down.
Weeds everywhere.
The path overgrown.

Turning in circles
kicking up leaves
I get mad at myself.

Lifting a branch
swinging it high
I hit the ground like it had a part
    in me staying in the house all this time.
I smack a tree next

then two more
crying all the while.

What use did it do you hiding inside?
Who did it help?
Nobody.
        Not Ma nor me.

Facing the lighthouse miles off
my feet pointed north
I wipe my chin and cheeks.
Not sure what to do.

TOGETHER AGAIN

When Hattie and her birds
catch up to me
she's out of breath.

Bent over
with a stick in my hand
I draw circles in the dirt
three
planets.

She asks if I'm ready.

No.

Am I going to the lighthouse
or back home?
She wants to know.

Can't say.
Ain't sure.

She don't say a word for a while.
Just watches me give Mars two moons.
Make people on Venus out of sticks.

"You nervous? Scared? Tired?" she asks.

I ain't got the words for how I feel.

Hattie sits on the ground next to me.
Puts my helmet on my head.
Sits shoes at my feet.

"Take your time, James Henry."

I know she don't mean it.

TROUBLE

Whenever the teacher is late for school
Hattie takes over.

She isn't fond of waiting.

With a eye on my handiwork, she says
"Come, James Henry. You'll see
I'm right about that old moon."

My stomach quivers.
Knots up.

Hattie stands.

I look over my shoulder
back the way we came
and there she is.

Lottie Jean.
Headed our way, fast as a train.

"He's coming!
He's coming!
He's coming!" she says, passing us.

RUNNING FOR OUR LIVES

We run
    one behind the other
        up a path no wider than a set of steps.
            Wobbling
                me anyhow
                    trying to stay upright
                        me anyhow
                            to not tip over into a dried-out creek
filled
                        with wet rotten leaves
                            that follows Mulberry Road like a
                shadow   till it joins the Pee
                Dee River
                      which empties
                        into the ocean a ways up
                            where the lighthouse
            sits.

BREATHE

Wet
from head to toe
soaked
we use our fingers like rags
wipe our faces
and necks
send
sweat
flying
quick as bees
hunting pollen

and don't quit running
        till we're standing in the middle of nowhere.

We're gonna die out here.

NOWHERE

North Carolina has more trees
than God got angels, Gran says.

    Redwoods
    sugar maples
    firs
    cedars
    gum trees.
Millions.

Gran swears
when slaves came
these same trees was standing
shading
praying over 'em
reaching for heaven
stomping the devil at the same time.

I'm sitting under a chaney ball tree, ruminating.

Sister's birds, truly free for once
flitter from tree to tree
singing
complaining
along with all the rest.

THE PLAN

Sister plots our next move.
We'll backtrack to Lottie Jean's house
change
into clean, fresh clothes
eat
spend the night
leave.

I look at Lottie Jean
then at Sister.

They can't go in dresses, they say.
There's rocks to be climbed
a flashlight to be had
hats to keep their heads cool.

It's a perfect plan, Lottie Jean says,
taking out something I didn't know she had.
The pouch filled with my wrappers.
She saw it on the table
thought it would bring me comfort.
Handing it over
she slips her arm through mine
tries to force me to stand.

"I can walk on my own!"

I tie the pouch to my belt.
Fold my arms and don't move.
Till Sister shares something
        she's never told me before.

"You think I can go off to school
with you forever inside the house?
No friends to speak of?
Ma and Daddy gone?"

I blink. Get to my feet.

She steps in closer
with a hug the size of Oklahoma.

"We're twins, Brother.
We gotta look out for each other."

I think about Ma and Uncle.
There's nothing he wouldn't do for her.

"Can you do this one thing for me, Brother?"
I start walking.

GONE FISHING

Spotting pond water
with mosquitoes for guards
    Lottie Jean runs ahead of us.

I look up and see something new.
One dark cloud.

What if it rains?
    And the water rises?
Who'll save Hattie?

I step back, still dripping wet.
Hide behind a tree.
And watch.

Sister spies the sky.
Skips across the grass
kicks off her shoes
looks back at me
runs to Lottie Jean.

A THIEF

We come across a field
next to a house
with clean clothes hanging on the line.

Lottie Jean swipes a dry shirt not my size
but for me anyhow.

If she had to smell me one more second
she'd faint, she says, fanning herself.

LOTTIE LEADS THE WAY

Lottie Jean looks left and starts walking
like she knows these parts.

Sister follows.

We go down a hill
running some because we gotta.

We pass a stone quarry
    filled with stagnant water
and logs
    put in to keep us kids from swimming in it
    going under
    never coming up.
    Gran and her friends fought for that.

The girls jabber on with me close behind
counting my wrappers.
They stop after a while
pull up orange poppies
roots and all.
Not bothered by dirt
falling on their clothes like rain.
Or mosquitoes eating me up.

A NEW KIND OF TROUBLE

I try to tell Hattie to slow down
wait up
take care because you never know
what might be lurking for you.

She rushes ahead anyhow
like she's been waiting to be free a long time.

Last to turn the bend
I find them two frozen stiff.

"Now what?" Lottie says
eyeing the trouble facing us.

THE APPLE WARS

The Baker brothers
ditch
apples
they were swiping
from a tree known for easy pickings
that branches out over the road.

Hattie steps ahead of us.
"Y'all boys go home now,"
she says in Gran's quiet after-church voice
    though it's Saturday.

An army of hellions,
Gran calls them Bakers—but never on Sundays.

Their cousin Red smiles.
Squints at the sky
blinks
like sand's been kicked in his face.
Not one to ever join in
he follows
like rain after thunder
once the others start walking our way.

The eldest Baker stops. Spits.
"Good to see ya, James Henry."

Hattie Mae takes off
running
disappearing in trees
a stone's throw away.

Sweat beads join one to the other
on their way down my nose,
dripping on my shirt like tears.

They're gonna kill me out here.

Sister returns with both hands full.

She's not the captain.
But she gives Lottie Jean orders.

"Hold tight to Brother's hand.
Don't let go. No matter what."

Lottie Jean does what she's told.

Hattie steps in front of me.
Lays one branch down
lifts the other high in the air like a spear.

Elbow to elbow
them Bakers stand in the road
six feet away or so
and laugh.

Not Red Baker, though.

"Hattie Mae"—
Titus, the eldest, does most of the talking—
"wears the britches."

Blu
second born
thinks I should be in skirts
wear a bonnet on my head.

Lottie Jean speaks on my behalf
not that I ask her.
"Leave him alone. He has seen
his share of troubles."

They dredge up what drowned in the ocean
pants I wore in
and the log that snagged 'em off
courage
I
took in with me but left behind
and Dog.

It's Ma's woes and Dog's loss
not the other
things I left behind
that set
me to tearing up.
It's no help to me
that Lottie Jean wipes a tear away.

Titus squeaks.
Calls me a coward
a mouse.
Blames Ma's situation on me.

Hattie flings the branch their way.
Claps at the sight of it hitting
Graham Baker upside the head
knocking him off his feet.

So, I guess you can say she starts the war.

LOSING COURAGE

The Bakers
four out of six anyhow
snatch apples off trees and the ground
hurl 'em our way one at a time
two and three at once
until Hattie's hunched over kneeling in the dirt
beside me and Lottie Jean
        more scared than I've ever seen her.

My mouth dries out
my lips itch.

Lottie Jean drops my hand
doubles over
covers her head with her bare arms.

Sister is my shield.
Grabbing another branch
she stands
throws
misses.

Pants and skirts are all the same to the Bakers.
Hands filled with apples
they come for us like elephants.

Dust
floats
flies
into our mouths and eyes
with every step they take
every move we make.

Coughing
I keep my eyes on the sky
and wonder
if I'll ever get my courage back.

NO CRYING

Lottie Jean jumps up
lifts her dress
runs like the dickens
into thickets and thorns
     that rip her hem and sleeves
but cannot stop her.

Hattie bends low
whispers in my ear.

She
is the captain
right now anyhow
so
I must do what I'm told.
"No questions asked."

She stands
straight and tall in the apple rain.
Me too.
No crying
no matter how much it hurts.
Those Hattie's words.

I do what I'm told.

ATTACK!

Hattie Mae tells her birds to go get 'em!

Nutcracker spreads his wings
leaves his spot
on top a weather vane
        stuck high on a barn up the road some.
He flies
dives over our heads
circles them Bakers
aims for Blu's face
claws out.

Blu turns chicken
runs.

Hattie Mae picks up apples
throws and misses.

Pullman finds Parker's scalp
pecks until he hollers.

Hattie claps. I cheer.

Them Bakers scatter like spilled seeds
cup their hands like nets to protect their heads.

Hattie eyes the trees over yonder and hollers
"Lottie Jean!"

Then looks my way when she gets no answer.

THE BAKERS STRIKE BACK

The Bakers don't take well to losing.
Who doesn't know that?

Seems like they can smell
when one or the other is in trouble.
Sure enough
out of nowhere
comes Bobbie Baker
with a rock in his hand.

Up it goes
flying higher than Nutcracker
falling
fast
catching his wing on its way down.

"Bull's-eye!"
a few Bakers say.

Nutcracker is on the ground
his neck twisted one way
his wing bent back
broken I suspect.

Sister screams.

I go back to the ocean.
The day Nutcracker led Uncle to me.

The Bakers fight on
all except Red Baker.
He walks through the apple storm
paying it no never mind.

Knee
by
knee
I get to my feet
shaking inside and out.

Only then do the apples stop.

Not me.
Nor the only Baker who never picked up a apple today.

Together we meet Sister in the middle.
"Sorry," he says.
"Our family wouldn't take to us killing birds."

I kneel.
"Hattie? You okay?"

Sister lifts
kisses Nutcracker
     her favorite.

"Will you help me bury him, Brother?"

I lead the way
not looking behind because
like Gran says
sometimes it's best
not to know what's gaining on ya.

BURYING TIME

Hattie claws the ground
sets her bird down.

After she speaks
she covers up what the Bakers
took from her
stabs the earth with
sticks to mark the spot.

Red Baker offers
his condolences again.
Warns us to get
        if we know what's good for us.

BACK WHERE I STARTED

I wanna go home.

Hattie won't leave Lottie Jean
to be found
by a bunch of hooligans
she says.

I look at the other Bakers
restless.

"What I ever do to them, Hattie?"

Red Baker's blue-black eyes follow mine.

"Dog was their favorite.
They think you are a coward."

Dog didn't belong to anyone or anything
except maybe those
kind enough to feed him
or the trees and leaves
that gave him shade
the Pee Dee River he cooled in
drank from.

My knees wobble some.
"Nobody owned him.
He just . . ."

Hattie looks at me
surprised
"Brother . . . you're . . . talking."

I cover my mouth.

STORM WARNING

Lottie Jean runs out the trees
rushes by us
never stopping.

"Run!"
she says.

We do like we're told
before we truly see what's got Lottie Jean
    so discombobulated.

A wolf.

NO SECOND CHANCES

Wolves and the Bakers
     don't give no second chances.
Hattie and me know that.
So
we three do like the Bakers and get
     fast as we're able.
Running in every which direction
quick as we can.

A LITTLE GOOD LUCK

For once
today anyway
something goes our way.
Wolf took a liking to them more than us.
Chases the Bakers
nipping at their heels the whole time.
Lottie
me
and Sister
get away clean.

"Hurray!" I say.
Till I notice Sister's condition.

NO MORE BRAVE

Is this my twin?
Brave Hattie.
Can't be.

Her cheeks are wet with tears.
She's crying over Nutcracker, she says,
tired
scared too
maybe.
Not herself at all,
I see.
Could be that's why
she won't move,
not one step,
no matter what me
or Lottie Jean says.

I'm thinking about the Bakers
when I take her by the arm
and start walking.
They got more reasons than ever to be mad at us.

A WAY OF ESCAPE

Before we clear the covered bridge
a wagon turns onto it.
What you know?

A way home.

WIDOWS AND WAGONS

Hattie and me know the rules.

Don't look white people in the eyes.
Say *yes sir*
no ma'am.
Be polite as ever you were.

"Afternoon," we three say at once.
The two widows live up the road from us.

The eldest sister always drives.
The other never talks. Just nods.

Lifting off her wide-brim straw hat
Miss Mamie wipes her brow with her arm.

"Ain't seen you out, boy, since . . ."
She thinks on it some.
Then names the month, day, and hour
she last set eyes on me.

I was soaking wet being carried in Gran's house by Uncle.
The whole time I heard him saying
    "Now don't you die on me, son."
    Wasn't till I recovered that he turned on me.

ONWARD

Miss Mamie questions me in particular
about the storm that must have drew me out.
"Is your grandmother under the weather?" she asks.
"Is your ma worse?"

"No ma'am," I say
following the rules.

I think about Ma.
The widows do too, I suppose.
Miss Mamie looks at me with them watery green eyes.
"She was a good woman.
Raised you children right nicely."

Sister rubs the horse's nose.

Says Ma is still Ma.
Just taking her time getting better.

How would she know?

Miss Mamie's sister nods.

Hattie Mae changes the subject always when it comes to Ma.
"Could we please get a ride to Lottie Jean's house, ma'am?"
With her hand covering her brow, she looks up.
"We'd be beholden, if you could."

They would, Miss Mamie says.
They're headed in the other direction though.
Uptown.
For supplies.

But if we don't mind the detour
   they'd get us there long before dark, they promise.

"That'll do," Sister says.

Miss Mamie snaps the reins.
Says come if we coming.

Her sister nods.

The horse starts walking
trotting like he's plumb tuckered out.

Miss Mamie
throws dried corn over her shoulder
into the back of the wagon.
Hattie's birds
thankful
greedy
flap their wings
go have lunch.

The girls get on next.
I stay put.

But no sooner than
the wagon pulls off
do them Bakers tumble into the road
fists up
their eyes promising us
this ain't the end of things.

With our feet hung over the back of the wagon
the three of us are quiet for a mighty long while.
So are the widows.

The wagon rolls up the highway
        rocks us like babies in cribs.
Lottie Jean's head
hung low
shakes back and forth while she naps in straw.

I keep watch, hold tight to my pouch
because you never know.

"Hattie,"
I whisper after a while.

"Yes, Brother."

"I hate cotton."

Her eyes open and she yawns.
"Sure is a lot, ain't it?"

It goes on forever, seems like.

"Ma hated it too," Hattie says.
"Picking cotton, I mean. Gran too."

The bolls cut ya fingers
make 'em bleed
the work bends your back near to breaking
leaves you poor as you started, Daddy would say.

"Which is why we have to get you back in school."
Sister yawns again.
Repeats Ma's words.
"Our people picked long enough.
Time for some others to do the picking."

TRAIN RIDE

Between the cotton fields
and the train tracks
there's the white widows and us
sweating our way up the road
stirring up dust.

Resting inside
their wings tucked tight
Hattie's birds lay in between her and Lottie Jean
both asleep.

I wanna sleep too
but the widows drive like
they're trying to beat the train to town.

I lift my arm high
pull it down four times quick
hoping the conductor will see me and give a toot.

He don't.

Black smoke puffs out the engine
leaves a trail of soot you could see from Triton, I bet.

Curled up beside Sister
my eyes almost closed
I see a noose hanging on a tree.

If them Bakers don't get you
the Knight Riders will.

"Hattie."
I nudge her

do my best to wake her.
She doesn't budge.

Miss Mamie says, real quiet like,
"Hand me that shotgun, boy,"
like she can see my face
read my mind
hear my heart beating a mile a minute.

Reaching under the straw
I pull out what they want.

Thankful.

PART 4

BAD THINGS HAPPEN

FOR THE CHILDREN

Gran warned us during visits
again once we came to live with her
"We ain't always wanted
even though we been here
three hundred years or more."

She gave us the rules.
Too many to remember.
Too important to forget.

Watch what we do with our eyes.
Watch what we say with our mouths.
Watch where our hands and feet go.
Come home alive.

Ma left the South the first time
because she said it was too much.
No way to live.
She came back for Gran.
Stayed for the children, she said.

UPTOWN

Out here in these parts
anything can happen.

So
when I stiffen up
freeze inside and out
like ice on Mars
I don't get mad at myself.

LEAVING THE WIDOWS BEHIND

The widows park behind the hardware store.
Remind us to mind our manners
stay close.

We do
for a while
then Hattie gets ideas.

There's a water fountain on Main.
"We'd like to get a drink," she says.
Miss Mamie nods this time.
Keeps on shopping.

Off we go
turning the corner
quenching our thirst at a fountain just for us.
Not the best.
But it's all there is.
Sister sneaks a drink from theirs.

Not far off
I see the train at the station
waiting.
Steam rising.

"What if them Bakers hitched a ride into town?"
I ask Sister.

She laughs.
Takes Lottie and me by the hand
swears our troubles are behind us now.

WATCHING

Stores
line both sides of Main Street.

Hattie
all smiles
rushes ahead of us.

It's useless,
I want to tell Lottie Jean,
to try to keep Sister away from
stores filled as full as the ones in Detroit
just not as fancy.

Window after window Sister
stares
at dresses with ruffles
handmade hats
ties for our dad
a big boot that swings
over the door.

I stay put
my hands in my pockets
my lips drying out
my eyes looking about
watching
everything that moves
because anything
could happen to us here.

NEVER FORGET

Hattie is in a hurry
which is why she forgets I suppose
not to forget to give whites the right-of-way
when they're walking on the same sidewalk as us
breathing the same air.

I been inside a long time
	but I still remember.

SAVING SISTER

A family with four kids head our way.
So does a man not far behind 'em wearing a tight suit
looking important
in a hurry.

Hattie's nose stays pressed to the window glass.
Lottie's too.
Sister's birds sit on the shoe sign watching.
I keep watch too.

The family, all blond, find a window to look into.
The man fingers his pocket watch
speeds up.

Maybe he's got a meeting to go to.
Maybe he's late for supper, I think.
Turns out I'm wrong.
There's something in the window
Sister and Lottie stand in front of
that he wants to see.
Only
        he doesn't want to wait his turn or
        share the window spot with them.

"Outta my way!" he says
like they're pesky flies bothering him.

Lottie steps aside.
Sister stays where she is.

Like Ma
        Hattie believes things

in the South aren't always fair.
Gran says Hattie has to learn when to strike
    when to hold her tongue.

His face turns red.
"Didn't you hear me, gal?"

Hattie stands tall and straight
like her feet are set in concrete
her ears stuffed with cotton.

I do like I did in the ocean.
Freeze. Stand still. Hope nothing bad happens to me.
He reaches over.
Squeezes her shoulder.
Sister raises her voice.
"I got as much right to—"

His hand goes up.

Lottie Jean
replaces me.
Apologizes for Sister.
Tells the man she's ignorant
poor
from the other side of the tracks.
"Which is why she's so ill behaved."

His hand finds his pocket.
Pulls out the watch again.
His eyes go from the watch to Sister
to Lottie to me.

"I thought as much."

Sister calls for her birds.

I get to her quick.
"We nearly lost Ma.
Daddy won't forgive me if we lose you too.
I couldn't forgive myself either."

I take Sister by the hand
and head for the drugstore.

GONE

We'd almost made it back to the widows
when Lottie Jean asked, "What's the hurry?

The widows are slow.
Even I can tell that," she said.

"Plus they have more stores to go to.
They said so themselves."

That's all Sister needed to hear.

I had to run to keep up with them.
I tried to warn 'em
while they dillydallied the day away.
But they knew better, they said.
Now
we're back and the widows are gone.

We look for them on this block and the next.
Can't find them anywhere.
Only their wagon tracks.

"What now?"
Lottie rubs her stomach.
Sits down on the ground.
"It's a long walk to my house.
        I'll die if I don't eat first."

RAGAMUFFINS AND RAIN

People would be more inclined,
to be charitable and kind to us, Lottie thinks,
if we were dressed decently and in order.
"Not like ragamuffins."

Gray dusty shoes
arms and legs too
we look like nobody loves us.
Our clothes are no better
our hair is disheveled, out of place
weighed down with the day's travels.

     I lick my parched lips
look up at the sky
see a dark cloud
for the second time today.

I tell Sister rain is due.

She never listens
Lottie Jean either.
They keep walking ahead of me.
Talking of things that don't include me
like all the letters Sister will write to Lottie Jean
once she's up north
attending that school.

NEW CLOTHES

We tiptoe
run sometimes
look over our shoulders
hope not to get caught trying to swipe clothes
to replace those we have on.

A woman with a broom chases us out her yard.
Brings us good luck anyhow.

At a church up the street
    we find what we need.

Clean clothes. A basketful.

THE END OF THE LINE

For the poor and needy
a sign stuck in the ground says.

We change
one behind the other
into shirts and pants just our size.
Leave our old things in a pile in the grass.

Now
we only need a few more items, Sister says.
"A flashlight, for starters.
You never know when you might need one."

We're nearly out the yard
      when we get caught.

A COOK AND A SMILE

His right hand holds tight to a pie pan.
His left
lifts a spatula up high.

"Just made." He smiles.
Reminds me of Gran
brown wrinkles everywhere.

In the grass
with our backs against a whitewashed fence
we eat slice after slice
drink ice-cold milk
try not to burp
me anyhow.

Cook looks at the sky.
"Rain's due.
And here ain't the place to be in the thunder and the dark."
He told that to other boys not too long ago, he says.

I look at Sister.
Lottie Jean asks for more pie.
Hattie Mae inquires about them boys.
"Did one look like his hair was on fire?"

"Could be he did.
Could be he didn't," Cook says
taking back his plates and forks.
"It's like colored children
is dropping out the sky
so many passed through today."

I jump up.
"We have to leave, Sister."

"Which way to the lighthouse?"
she asks Cook.

Lottie looks surprised.
"You mean my house."

Sister says she was thinking while she ate her pie.
Now that we got clean clothes
she figures we might as well finish
what we started.

Cook shakes his head.
Says there's nothing good for us there.
"Didn't you hear about the lady that nearly drowned?
Pity."

We don't try to explain.

NAP TIME

We don't mean to nap
it's the pie that does it.

We parked ourselves in a park to rest some
talked about the Baker brothers and their cousin.
Sister's right I suppose.
Those boys Cook saw couldn't be them.
How would they get here? Walk?

"It's too far by foot," she told us.

Then
one by one
we dozed off.
I was the last to go.

I'll just nap for a little while,
I told myself right before my eyes shut.

Now it's dark.

LIGHTNING STRIKES

Sister darts across the grass
fussing at her birds and us—like
the dark is our fault.

"How can we get through the woods
to the lighthouse without a flashlight?"
I ask.

"We can't," Lottie Jean says.

Sister pays us no never mind.
Says we have what we need.
"Stars and a moon overhead.
Plus you, James Henry."

Just like that lightning strikes
turns the dark inside out.

For a minute
it looks like morning.

I'm the first to start running
saying we need to get outta here.

LEFT BEHIND

Rain
bringing thunder with it
comes down in sheets.

Before Hattie can clap for her birds
we're soaked
from our heads to our toes.

Running past farms and houses
clotheslines and churches
we find what we're searching for
stop where we started.

Main Street.
Every store is closed.
Every streetlight is out.
No one is around except us
we think.

Then I see it.
The wagon.
I point.
"Look, Hattie Mae.
They waited!"

We run fast as we can.
Their wagon is faster.

Pulling off Main Street
trying to outrun lightning
it's gone before we get to it.

Lottie Jean sneezes.
"Achoo."
Tells us this is the worst
day of her life.

I start crying.

DOING SOMETHING TO HELP

Wet as a crocodile
tears still in my eyes
I walk up to a store with a sign in the window
shouting who's welcome and who ain't.

Down on my knees
I crawl in the mud
go under the porch.
Tell Sister and Lottie Jean to come.

We'll stay drier here
get some sleep
head for the forest
        once the sun comes up
I tell 'em
still shaking like a leaf.

Sister has her own ideas.

OPEN DOORS

Hattie Mae goes from store to store.
Turns knobs.
Doesn't stop
till one does what she wants.

I warn Sister not to go in.

STRANGE BIRDS

Lottie Jean sneezes. "Achoo."
Follows Hattie Mae into the store.

I stay put.

Soaked
down to my underwear
I bite on my nails
pray
keep my eye on Hattie's three birds.

Thunder
pounds
sounds like bombs dropping.

Pullman and the rest take off
like hunting dogs is chasing after 'em.

Running
I follow
try to round 'em up like chickens.

Around the corner
near a stable
I hear people talking.
Walking close by.

"Over there.
Shout if you find 'em."

I remember that voice.
It's him
the man with the pocket watch.

RUN, SISTER, RUN

"Run," I say back at the store.

Sister wipes chocolate off her chin.
Lottie Jean trips on her way out.

"This way," I say,
falling facedown on Cranberry Lane.
Sister
out of breath
steps ankle-deep in a ditch full of mud
loses a shoe
plus the flashlight she found in the store.

I pick up what I can.
Her left shoe.

Lottie Jean
sneezing again
never stops
passes me and Sister soon enough.

Turning around
I see two men gaining on us
one
with a rifle in his hand.

DON'T STOP

Running this way and that
we get a ways ahead of them.
Hattie slows down some.
Cries.
Because none of her birds are with us.
I put my wet hand in hers.
Lottie Jean does the same.

"We can't stop, Hattie," I say.
"Not for nothing or nobody."

WHO IS THIS HATTIE MAE?

"Keep going."

She surprises me
hands my words back to me.
    "I . . . I . . . I . . . can't."

Sister turns into a stubborn mule
plants her feet
refuses to move
even though the woods are just a scratch away.

FOOLS

Still coming.
Getting closer and closer
they don't give up.

I eye the sky
imagine myself on the moon
a lasso in my hand
swinging down to earth
hog-tying those men.

Lottie Jean begs Sister to get moving.

I ask Hattie
if she wants us to get filled with buckshot
strung up tonight.

She walks up to the forest door
with the two of us beside her.

Only a fool would go in there this time of night.

REIGN FOREST

At night
Reign Forest is as black
as five widows
dressed in black
riding in a Model T at midnight
Gran is fond of saying.

I look up at the moon
with clouds doing their best to swallow it up.

"How will we make it through there?"
Lottie Jean asks.

Sister talks brave.
"We can do anything," she says.
"Didn't we whip them Baker boys?"

Not exactly.

Her fingers squeeze mine near to breaking
telling the truth about things.

"Ouch!"

Lottie Jean whispers,
"I'm not . . . not sure I can do this."

Crickets
        a million I bet
and frogs

Sister's and my least favorites
call us like they do back home.

I lie. "We'll be okay."

Together we hop into the forest like scared rabbits.

NO TURNING BACK

Soon as we start
we stop.

Blink.
Blink.
Blink.

Try to get our eyes used to the dark.

Blink.
Blink.
Blink.

Take one step.
Blink again.
It's still dark, though.
Mud
giants

everywhere.

But at least the rain stopped.

TREES

Bony long arms
twisted like snakes
tap my shoulder
scratch my neck
get tangled in Sister's
and Lottie's hair.

Hattie stops.
Covers her eyes.
Scared
Sister says she can't take another step.
Lottie agrees.

I tell them we on a planet
never seen by humans before.

Couldn't think of nothing better.

Lottie Jean holds my arm tight as night holds stars.
"You're not afraid, James Henry?"

I lie.
Talk to Sister, not her.

"All the time
I was on the roof
I was getting stronger
braver."

Truth is, I was doing no such thing.

They'll know once I faint.

OPPOSITES

"Open your eyes."

"I can't."

"Sure, you can," I tell Sister.

"No, I can't."

"One eye at a time."

"No."

"I'm the captain, Hattie Mae!
Do like I say!"

She opens one eye.

"Good."

Almost breaking my fingers
she opens her right eye next
blinks both eyes
opens 'em wider.

"Ready?" I say.

Sister takes a big breath.
"Aye, aye, Captain."

Lottie Jean points. "Which way?"

One path gets erased by the dark.
The other's no better.
It goes straight a few feet
disappears in the night like a hand in a pocket.

I'm not sure which direction to go.
So I sniff
try to smell and hear the Pee Dee River
which leads to the ocean
where the lighthouse stands.
I don't want to accidently end up in it tonight.

"Hush," I tell Sister.

"Hush," I tell Lottie,
humming to quiet her nerves.

It's hard with everything wet here
with other sounds all around us
but I think I smell the river
hear the river
washing over rocks
rolling and dipping
in a hurry
full after tonight's feeding
        waiting
for us to show ourselves in the morning.

"This way," I say
walking through weeds up to my knees
heading in the other direction.

HAPPY TEARS

Not far up the path
Hattie's birds find us.

Sister's crying again.

BRAVE DON'T LAST ALWAYS

Trees creak like floors
sound sad as Gran after she first saw Ma and me that night.

Animals we can't see talk to each other
hurry up trees
show us their eyes but hide their bodies.

Something howls
sounds big as a cow or a horse
the size of an elephant.

I feel like I'm sinking inside myself
like my throat is closing
and all the brave in me
is sliding out like snot from my nose.
I stop cold.
"Hattie . . . I . . . I just can't."

Her and Lottie Jean stand still as rocks.
Hold tight to each other
and pray.

DIRECTIONS

Hattie's birds take over
lead the way.

Forest birds
all around us
invisible in the dark
call out like they're giving directions.

A BED OF THEIR OWN

Sister always said her birds were smart.
Flying no further than it takes to get from
the back of our house to the front
they stop at a tree.

A hole in the trunk big enough to hold two
        plus Hattie's birds
will be their bed tonight.

Using my hand for a ladder
Hattie climbs up
crawls in
with Lottie Jean close behind.

"Achoo," Lottie says, sitting next to Sister.
"It's damp in here. Wet."
Scratching and slapping herself
she complains about bugs biting
spiders on her arms.

Sister shivers.
Says we'll take turns staying awake
keeping watch.
"Give James Henry time to rest."

I stomp my foot.
Stand straight and tall.
Salute.
"I'm the captain. I don't need sleep.
I don't even like it," I say,
wondering what's out there that I can't see.

GUARD DUTY

Standing guard
I search the sky.
Ignore the clouds
look for three stars
Vega
Deneb
Altair—
the Summer Triangle.
Easy enough to find if you know what to look for.

SOMETHING OUT THERE

Snap.

What's that?
Those men?
The Bakers?

    I look around for a hiding place.

"Hoo, hoo, hoo."

    Press my hands to my ears
    stand tall and rock.

Ka-ca!
Ka-ca!
Ka-ca!

    Backing up
    I bump
    into Hattie and Lottie Jean's tree
hold still
    hold myself
    hoping not to go on myself.

MINE

I go find my own tree.

ALONE

Wide as our outhouse
branches reaching everywhere
this tree touches all the trees it can

maybe so they won't be scared.
(I'm scared.)

I jump once
twice
six times.
Hang on to the lowest branch and don't let go.

Kick.
Swing.
Sit.

Those are my father's words
not mine.
Remembering them
I end up sitting on a limb
higher than the one I started on.

Again, and again,
like I was taught by him and Ma.

Two stories up
bugs all over me
I see a skittish brown squirrel
        jump tree to tree
sap oozing off bark
birds

including Hattie's
spying on me.

You gonna fall.

I swallow
close my eyes
lay my chest on the tree's arm
hold on for dear life.

Breathe.

"Breathe."

    I
    do
    like
    I
    tell
    myself
    let
    out
    one
    breath
    take
    one
    in.
    Do it again and again.

"Open . . . open your eyes."

    I
    do

then undo
  then do it again.
My heart slows some.

Not my mind, though.
It likes pestering me.

But higher is better
safer.
Wolves can't get to you, I think.
Neither can fat old men.

STARS

I sleep some.
Watch for those men sometimes too.
See the sky clear up
thousands of stars
        winking at me.

When my eyes finally close again
I take off for the twenty-fifth century.
Destination Mercury
where I'll build my own colony.

PART 5

OFF TO THE
LIGHTHOUSE

RISE AND SHINE

Bright enough to hurt my eyes.
White.
Hot as fire.
The sun feels like it's within spitting distance
instead of ninety-three million miles away.

Sweating
I look down but stay put.

Try to get my bearings
listen to my stomach growl.

Gran started making breakfast a hour ago
when the sun came up.

Sister and me would be stirring in our beds still
washing soon
like the raccoon nearby licking itself
not concerned with me at all.

I close my eyes.
See Gran at the stove
        flipping hotcakes
frying more bacon than we could eat.

"Send some to them Baker boys"
        she'd say before the accident.

Ma liked that.
Me too then.

HEADED DOWN

There must be two million
birds in here.
All singing and talking.
Sounding happy.

Standing
like there's earth beneath my feet
I start down
fall soon enough.
Get stabbed and scratched along the way.

Sister screams
along with Lottie Jean and me.

One branch knots my head
the next stops my fall.
I end up belly down
holding on.

"Don't move."
It's Lottie Jean.

"I'm coming for you!"
Sister starts climbing.

"No! I . . . I . . . need to rest," I say.

For once
Hattie Mae does things my way.

ON OUR WAY

Down below
it starts again.
My hands shaking.
Me nervous about everything.

"Hurry up,"
I tell Sister and Lottie Jean.

Looking behind more than ahead
I wonder if they're here
still chasing us
them Bakers, those men.

Sister and Lottie talk while we walk.
Scratch.
Mostly they complain.

But who ain't hungry
tired
half wet still?
Scared.

FOLLOW THE RIVER

Ma always said
the river is a finger
pointing to the lighthouse.

We
follow the edge of the river
close as a beard follows a chin.

Avoid grass that's too soggy
make detours when we need to.
Stick together.

Listening
to one another's stomach's growl.

FOOD

I pluck the head off a worm.
Sit the rest on a mushroom
and eat.

Hattie Mae and Lottie Jean
take off screaming.

Six more worm sandwiches later
my stomach quiets some.

Not my mind, though.
We lost about two hours
searching
for food they won't eat.

DOING WHAT WE HAVE TO

Lottie kneels
feels the ground
follows my advice finally.

Animals carry more than they can eat
I told her by accident.
Berries
seeds
twigs for cleaning teeth.

"Ill," she said at first.
"I just couldn't, James Henry."

I find a patch of dandelions.
Snap the tender green stems.
"Eat
but not too many," I say to Sister for Lottie's sake.
"They can be bitter."

Lottie Jean pulls a few out the ground.
Sniffs.
Closes her eyes.
Bites.
Spits 'em out.
Sister says we'll need a gardenful
to fill bellies full.
Goes to find something on her own.

"James Henry. Wineberries!"
Lottie meets her near thickets and vines.
Together they eat till their tongues change colors.
And their thirst goes away
for now anyhow.

I turn a branch into a walking stick
and protection.
Eat along the way.
Stop.
Wait for a snake
six inches long
as yellow as a canary
to go by.
Listen to a woodpecker working
hummingbirds humming

Sister saying she hopes she didn't eat too much.

Rubbing my eyes
I think about Gran
hope she ain't too mad
worried
sad
over us and our shenanigans.

Moving on
I find another worm, three.
Pluck off their heads.
Sit 'em between chick weed leaves.
Eat
Swallow
Repeat.

"No thanks,"
Hattie and Lottie Jean say,
looking disgusted.

A LONG WAY TO GO

Sister asks why I'm so quiet.
I stare at Lottie walking beside her.
Then look back the way we came
at
miles of grass
miles of trees
more in front of us.

"Maybe this wasn't such a good idea, Sister."
I look up.

Lottie Jean goes left to the river.
Dips her fingers.
Cools off her face and arms.
Sister does the same.
Returns.
Pats my hot face with her wet hands.
Promises
everything will be okay.

I face the river.
Think about the ocean.
Try not to think about the ocean.
Hold tight to my pouch.

DO SOMETHING

"No."
Lottie Jean takes a seat on a stump.
"I won't walk another step."

Sister goes over to her.
    She's on her side now.
Folding her arms
Hattie Mae says we've been walking in circles.
She knows
because she's seen this stump before,
she tells us.
"Twice now."

Lottie Jean swears
they'll find our bones out here.

Do something, I hear Ma say.
I tried that night and failed.

AT THE TOP OF THE WORLD

I scratch a itch on my nose.
Lottie Jean throws more questions my way.
"Can you see the lighthouse from up there?"

Not yet.
But
I could if I climb higher, I bet.
So
that's what I do.
I would climb to clouds
to the moon
never come down
if I could.

Two branches higher
not so steady this time
I wobble
hold on to the tree and point.

"I see it. I do."

I don't mention the ocean.
How light my head feels
my fingers shaking
slipping
on the branches.

You're gonna fall.

Sister says for me to come down—"now!"
Lottie Jean asks why she's so skittish.

"Seems to me James Henry is extremely good at this."

Sister is determined, she tells Lottie, to get me to the lighthouse
alive and in one piece.
"He nearly fell out that other tree, remember?"

I remember, so I hold on tighter.
Feel
wineberries making their way up my throat.

Hattie starts up.
I stop her.

Come down quiet as I can.

MORE QUESTIONS

It takes Sister a while to ask
    if I saw those men while I was up there.

"No."

"What about them?"
I know who she means.

The Bakers weren't nowhere to be seen either.
Not on the river.
Not in trees.
Nor on the ground walking around.

"Then
we don't have anything to worry about," says Lottie Jean.

CLEANING UP

For once I agree with Lottie.

The three of us smell something horrid
look worse still.

So
into the river they go
dancing and playing.

Lottie Jean ends up on Sister's shoulders.
Jumps off.
Goes under.
Swims in circles.

I stay back
watch the sky
watch out for trouble.
It always finds us.

Using their hands
they grab at fish
chase butterflies
laugh more of the day away.
Eat up hours.
I count my wrappers

Not that it matters.
The moon won't be out for a long, long time.

BEES AND OTHER TROUBLING THINGS

Sunning on their stomachs
they talk more of the day away.
Braid each other's hair
using their fingers for combs.
Rest.
Till Lottie Jean screams at the top of her lungs.

"My hair!"
She smacks her head with both hands
        like it's on fire.

"It's buzzing. They've got me."
Lottie hops around.
Runs in circles.
Heads for the Pee Dee River.
Jumps in.
Dunks herself over and over and over again.

Sister stays in the spot she started in
fighting
losing.

When I get to her
there's ground bees in her hair
crawling up her neck
stuck to her arms
stinging her all over.

Brave Hattie
doesn't say a word.
Just keeps fighting.

I fan and swat and slap 'em.
Pick 'em off Sister like ticks.
Take her by the hand
        take off running.

Knee-deep in the river, I wash her clean.
Turn to Lottie Jean next.

"James Henry,"
        Sister hollers,
once they're both free.
"Look.
You're in the water."

I feel the river moving
sand
under my shoes
trying to sink me.

"Don't let me drown, Hattie."

Sister takes my hand.
Holds on tight.
Walks with me.

Inside
I'm a gazelle
running
faster than the speed of light.

LOTTIE'S HERO

Lottie Jean makes a fuss over me.

"You saved me, James Henry."
She gives me a big smooch on the cheek.

    "Sister, tell her not to do that."

Sister swears I'm blushing.

Sitting under trees
we pick stingers out of each other
listen to the river.
Use cool mud to soothe our bites.

We look a worse sight than when we started.

"Hattie Mae?"

"Yes, Brother."

"I ain't been in the ocean or the river since that day."

"I know."

"This time I didn't think about Ma at all.
Is that wrong?"

"No."
Sister kisses my other cheek.

"And I ain't run.
I wanted to. But I didn't."

"That old blue moon is working already, is all."

HAPPY BIRTHDAY, LOTTIE JEAN

"Minute by minute your luck improves, James Henry.
    Mine diminishes."
A wasp stung Lottie Jean a little while ago.

"Soon I won't have any luck at all.
Though I ought not be surprised."

She jumps a log.
Scratches what itches.

"I was hoping to improve my lot by my birthday."

Sister stops in her tracks.
"Birthday! When?"

"In a few weeks."

In a blink there it is.
A mud pie
tall as Gran's coconut cakes
just as wide.

With broken sticks in the middle
leaves on the sides
it brings a smile to Lottie's mouth.

She claps.
Gives thanks.

Sister sings the birthday song.
Her birds join in.

"See, Lottie Jean. Your luck is already improving.
I wish you
ten new dresses for your birthday," Hattie says.

Sister asks me to add a birthday wish to hers.

I wish Lottie Jean
more luck
than even the Milky Way can hold.
Not that I say it out loud.

Sister looks disappointed.

SUN TIME

Before we started out this morning,
I checked the time.
For Lottie Jean's sake
I do it again
to prove
what I said was true
we've been walking sunning funning
sipping from the river six hours now.
Got a lot more time to go.

Lottie Jean only trusts
clocks and watches
to give the time.
I use my
hands and eyes.
Press
my fingers tight
fold in my thumb.
Turn my hand on its side
stretch out my arm
then close one eye
so
I only see the edge
of the bottom of the sun.

Down my hand goes
four tight fingers at a time
until it reaches the horizon.
I
count
every step my hand takes on the way down.
Add up that number
and get the time.

SWORD FIGHTS AND OTHER FUN

We duck behind trees
pluck leaves off limbs
make swords
duel.

With my helmet under my arm
I lead the way.
Point out strange animals on this planet.
Tell the girls what stars are made of.

Lottie says it's nonsense.
    "Everyone knows God put 'em up there."

A little while later
we hear someone laughing,
water splashing.

Hiding
spying
we get a good look.
It's Cook.
Wresting fish out the river with a rod.
Frying more in a pan
over red-hot flames.

Lottie heads his way.
Then Sister.
I'm the last to go.
After filling our stomachs with food
and all the lemonade we can drink
Cook packs up.
Tells us to come along before our luck runs out.

"We just couldn't."
Sister stands next to me.
Lottie Jean does too.

Cook fixes his eyes on me.

Lottie speaks up. "We can't.
But we thank you for your hospitality."

He gets in his boat
goes about his business
leaving us a little something behind,
        two soft peaches
        crackling fried just right.

NO MORE WRAPPERS

I hadn't noticed.

Lottie Jean did, of course.

My pouch is gone
along with the wrappers.

It must've come off in the river.

Sister says maybe I lost it
while we were chasing each other.

They're gone
that's all I know.
Along with my chances of winning.

For a while
I'm so sad
so mad
I fall on the ground
kick up dirt
wish I had never left home.

BAD LUCK AGAIN

Picking fish from between our teeth with sticks
moving slow as snails
we hear it.

People talking.
Heading this way.

"It's them," Sister says.
"Those men."

Lottie Jean drops her toothpick
stands as near to Sister as skin.
I'm next.

In a circle
our backs facing each other's
we shake
wait
listen.

"We can't outrun 'em twice,"
I whisper to Sister.

"Hattie Mae," Lottie Jean says under her breath.
"How can we get rid of bad luck if it keeps showing up?"

TITUS BAKER AND HIS REDHEADED COUSIN

And just like that there they are
two Bakers coming closer and closer
which is better than four or more of 'em I guess

especially if they're planning on beating the stuffing outta you.

BACK TO CAPTAIN

Sister bends low
picks up a branch and swings it.

"Don't," Lottie says. "He's hurt."

It could be a trick
Hattie Mae tells her.
"You can't trust those Bakers, you know."

I know.
Not Lottie, though.
Scratching her bumpy scalp
she goes to them.

Hattie
makes herself the captain again
tells me to get behind her.
I climb up high
I climb a tree high as I can
        and watch.

SQUEAK

"Come on, Titus Baker," Sister says.
"Let's have it out once and for all."

Red Baker steps in front of his cousin.
He never does that. No one does.

"Hattie Mae. Please . . . don't."
He points to Titus's foot.

Lottie asks how it got that way.

"Titus stepped on a rabbit trap." It's Red.
"Yelled something fierce
    when his foot got snapped."

"Shut up!" Titus says.

Sister circles them.
Says she's still got her doubts.
    "Who chased you into the forest?"

    Three men.
White.
That's all they know.

"How'd you get to town?"

They hopped a ride on a wagon, same as us.
Found themselves as wanted as we were.
Hid.
Had their fill
    eating fresh-baked blackbird pie
        stolen from a window ledge.

Red rubs his belly.
Wishes for more to eat.
Lottie hands him the last of our food.
Titus too.

It was that pie that caused all the trouble,
Red says, biting into a peach
licking his fingers
same as his cousin.

Those men came searching after them.
Found 'em among the dogwood trees
stuffed full.

They outran 'em.
But not the trouble that followed.

Sister drops the stick.

I look at Lottie.
Red shakes his head
stares at Titus's bloody foot
held together using his undershirt for a tourniquet.

Squeak.
I say it to myself.
Wait for it to sneak outta Titus's mouth any minute now.

Only it don't.

"Could ya . . . please help me?" he says under his breath.
"I won't make it without extra arms and legs."

Captain Hattie walks away.
I climb down
hurry by him.

If I didn't know better
I'd say Titus Baker was crying.

BEFORE THEN

Helios
is the Greek word for sun.
That's where the word *helium* comes from
Ma said one day in class.

Titus couldn't catch his breath
couldn't stand still
he had so many questions.

Red said he talked all the way home.
Shared more than he shoulda
    including Ma's plans to get him in his right grade.
His daddy pulled him out of school once he heard.

"'Cause helium can't help bring in no crops,"
his father told Ma.
"Neither can that Mr. Galileo man."

Ma never saw Titus cry before then.

MULTIPLICATION LOTTIE'S WAY

Lottie Jean is between me and Sister.
"Doesn't he look sad?"

Hattie Mae and me keep walking.

"And couldn't we
use some company along the way?" Lottie says.

"No." It's Sister.

Hattie Mae reminds her that the Bakers are headed home.
And
we're on our way to the lighthouse.

Lottie Jean's got other ideas.
"We can lead them out the forest
let them find their way from there."

Sister says what I'm thinking.
"Some girls court bad luck.
And you are one of 'em, Lottie Jean."

That's when Lottie asks what our mother would do.

Hattie Mae stops in her tracks.
Tells Lottie how fond Ma was of Titus.
How much he liked her in return.

Lottie hooks her arm through mine.
"Day by day our troubles have been multiplying.
Maybe doing good by him will put an end to it."

THANKFUL FOR SMALL THINGS

I'm
the
last
one.

In between
it's
them
three.

Sister is up front.

Lottie Jean kicks sticks out the way
sings now and then
asks if I'm okay.

I am as long as Titus Baker's foot
ain't worth a plug nickel.

SOMEBODY ELSE'S TURN

He's got nothing to say.
Not a word.

But since Ma's accident
he hasn't shut his mouth
not when it comes to me anyhow.

"Squeak."

"Coward."

That's what he'd say
like it was my name.

Is it his turn now?

Hattie always could read my mind.

"Titus Baker is a big old baby," she says, smiling.
"It's about time he got his."

TITUS BAKER'S TROUBLES

He can't walk too far or too long.
That's why
more often than we ought we stop.

I find a bush to hide behind.
Titus finds a tree
leans awhile
sits on a rock
     when he can't stand standing no longer.

I close my eyes
wishing
I had a rocket ship
to take me away
or nerve enough to run home
even if Uncle's there.

Because I don't trust this Titus
any more than I trusted the one with the good foot.

SCRATCHING MY HEAD

He cries
now and then
hides his face in his arm.
Same as me on the sand
in the ocean
and the dark
searching for Ma.
I almost feel sorry for him.

ANYHOW

Starting up again
we fan ourselves with our hands
 except for Lottie Jean, who uses her hair.

We swallow spit when we can't stop for water.
Come out our clothes
shirts anyhow
the boys do anyhow
those two anyhow.

Their shirts get tied around their heads
to stop sweat from rolling in their eyes
down their chins
onto their necks and chests.
It don't work so well.

I keep my helmet on.
Keep my eyes on him.
Carry a stick just in case.
Hattie's rules.

"Captains in space are always prepared,"
she said a little while ago.

"And remember, James Henry,
I'll be in a new school soon
so
you'll have to learn to protect yourself."

But what if he's joshing?
"What if he stomps me
beats me into the dirt while you're at school?"

Hattie calls for her birds.
They circle him
scare him
stop him from walking any further.

For the first time, his fist goes up.

FLIES AND FLOWER GIRLS

Lottie Jean runs up to us.
How do we like her hair? she asks, out of breath.

There's honeysuckle stuck in it
on purpose I guess
and sticks
on purpose I guess.

Grinning
she brings up Red Baker
who looks worn down
at the end of his rope.

"He's the best Baker of all, don't you think?"
Lottie Jean smiles at Hattie.

Sister agrees.
Leaves
comes back with sage in her hair,
along with a Carolina lily
orange
sprinkled with brown spots.

Titus Bakers fights off flies.
His foot far worse than when we started.

"I can't take it." He stops. Almost falls.
"I'm hot and dirty and—"

Red Baker hurries to the river
comes back with his shirt dripping wet.
Squeezes water on his cousin's head and foot

into his mouth next.
Tells Titus that everything will be all right.

Titus's eyes find mine every time.
For once he don't say a thing to me.
Just moans.

TAKING HIS TIME

One whole hour later
Titus Baker still sitting on that rock.

BUYING WHAT OUGHT TO COME FOR FREE

It don't stop, Reign Forest.
It goes on so long
seem like we won't ever make it out.

We pass a waterfall.
Walk slower than ever.
Quit talking to each other,
        all of us except Lottie Jean.

She tells Sister another bad-luck story.
That her mother divorced her father.
"The day after my birthday."

"Sorry to hear it,"
Red Baker says.

Her and the Dentist left New York City after that.
Left two other cities they moved to up north.

"Did you know you can't outrun bad luck?"
she asks Titus.

He hangs his head.
Stares at his foot.

"I know."

"Or give enough dresses away to make it leave?"

Sister gets extra quiet.

A family of white-tailed deer cross our path.
Sister whispers like they might hear.
"You can't buy friendship, Lottie Jean.
Not for all the money in the world."

"You don't say." Lottie smiles.

NO GOING BACK

Titus trips over a log he meant to step over.
Falls
gets helped up by Red and Lottie Jean
ain't grateful at all.

He blames me and Sister for his troubles.

"If my leg wasn't hurt, Hattie Mae, I'd—"

Sitting on a stump, he breaks a stick in two.
"Soon as I'm all fixed up, I'll fix you good
that coward brother of yours too."

His eyes find mine every time.
"Squeak."

"Titus Baker!"
Lottie Jean hurries over to him.
"You're just plain evil!"

She wipes her mouth and sneezes.
"We've been
        nothing but kind to you and—"

Folding her arms, she turns to me.
"I did it again, didn't I, James Henry?
I conjured up
drug in
more bad luck for us."

She apologizes to Sister and me.

Sister bends down.
Goes hunting for stones.
Fills her pockets full.
"If you don't leave my brother alone—"

I think about Gran's words.
Hattie Mae, you can't fight his every battle.

I fill my pockets and start walking.

"Hattie Mae," I say, "it's getting late.
Come if you're coming."

Those are Ma's words.
The ones she used when she was done
arguing
pushing
encouraging
us to do what needed doing.

"And y'all keep moving.
I'm the captain.
I make the rules."

Behind me
I see Titus's eyes with knives in 'em.

But he sets to walking anyhow.
With me leading the way.

LOTTIE JEAN'S SECRET

His foot
toes and all
is swollen
blue
filled with pus.

Ma's lips turned colors in the cold water.
Pink first, red, and then blue.

"That's a bad sign," I whisper to Sister.

"I know."

I sit on a rock long and wide as a car
watch them semicircle around Titus.

"James Henry." It's Lottie Jean.
"You okay?"

I don't answer her.
I answer to myself
in my head.
Yes.

"Not me."

She picks leaves out her hair
drops 'em on the ground on her way to me.

"I keep thinking that we'll never get out of here.
And that blue moon will come and go without us."

The moon is everywhere, I say to myself.
Trouble too.

She starts walking when I do.
Telling me about the time she went
skating on a lake and fell in.

"I almost drowned. But worse than that
was almost losing my cousin Helen.
She was six."

I turn to stone.
Swallow.
See Ma and Dog fighting water.
Going under
coming up coughing
swimming but not getting nowhere
fighting to live.

"It was awful," Lottie says,
putting her hand in mine.

I don't know how long it takes
for me to find the words.
But it seems like forever.

"It was," I say.
"Nobody knows how bad.
Not even Hattie Mae."

Lottie Jean whispers.
"I do . . . a little. Don't you think?"

I nod my head yes.
And for the first time, I talk about that night.

How scared I was.
The cold freezing water.
Swimming
but not getting anywhere.
The lightkeeper asleep in the watch room.

TAKING TURNS

We take turns
letting him lean on our shoulders
giving Red a rest now and then.

We'll get further that way
not leaving it to one person
to shoulder his burden. Even me.

Titus don't like it much
me being who I am plus shorter than him.

"But you needs all of us, not just one," Red says.
"Who can't see that?"

A little while later
I'm the one who stops.

I pull off my shirt
head for a tree with sap running free.

"Don't—"
Titus says with fear in his eyes.

Did I look like that when Ma was going under?

Sister tells him it won't hurt.

I
kneel.
Spread sap on his foot to seal the wound
take off, rip up my undershirt
rewrap his foot.

Hattie finds wood to make a brace.
Red stomps spiders that came with it.

I hold the planks in place.
Red wraps rags around 'em.
Ties Lottie's ribbons on for good measure.

"Better?" Lottie asks him.
Titus stands. Almost smiles at me.

MAKING EYES AT LOTTIE

He looks at her
but not the way he looks at us.
Smiles
not for long because the pain won't let him.
Holding on to his arm
Lottie behaves
like this was any ordinary day.

TICKTOCK

The sky is a clock
a pocket watch
ticktock.
It'll tell you when to plant corn or tobacco.
When rain, locust, or drought is due
high tides too.

Sailors knew like Gran knows like I know
look to the sky
the planets the moon or the sun
for the best time
the right day or month
to do what needs done
like sail to the other side of the world
plant a juniper tree for somebody you love
get to the ocean in time to catch the moon working.

I sets my watch by things above.
It ain't quit ticking on me yet.
Those Gran's words.

ALMOST TIME

Lottie points.
We stand still and enjoy the show
the sun going
from white to yellow
     then orange to red.

"It seems bigger than when
we started out this morning," Lottie says.

It's an illusion, I wanna tell her.
The nearer the sun gets to the horizon
the bigger it looks.
That's because objects around it
trees
barns
bridges
us
are so much smaller in comparison.

Sister whispers in my ear.
"Tell her.
I know you know the answer."

Red says he'd like to hear.
Standing tall, I tell 'em.

"You are the smartest boy in Seed County,"
Lottie shouts.

Seems like everything in the forest seconds her.

STILL WAITING

All around us
they talk about us
happy to have us leaving soon I bet.

We keep walking.
    And walking.
      Scratching our bites.
      Sweating.
Looking up a lot.

Close as leaves on a tree
we whisper.
Hear the river whispering too.
Happy to join the ocean soon I suppose.

Then like magic
the moon is out.
Bright.
Gigantic.
A sight to see.
High up in the atmosphere.
Full.
Just what I need.

"It don't look real,"
Titus says.

Hattie stands beside me.
Lottie Jean to my left.
"It looks like the most beautiful thing
I've ever seen in my whole doggone life," Lottie says.

GOODBYE, REIGN FOREST

Leaving Reign Forest
I think about the contest.
Meeting Buck Rogers.
He'll pick the typical American boy
in six more weeks.
I'd never be able to collect enough wrappers in time.

"Everyone knows.
That contest was mine to win."
I shake my head.

Hattie Mae's warm arm goes around me.
"You already won, Brother.
        Because you're here—see?"

She points to the lighthouse.
The ocean.
The moon
the sky
black
covered with stars millions of miles away
watching us.

"Now all we have to do is get to the lighthouse."

That's not true.
Titus Baker is still with us.

WHAT TO DO NOW?

Sometimes
a car drives by with folks like us in it.
    Not one's gone by since we been here
at the side of the road.

Lottie Jean thinks we ought to wait till one comes.
Red Baker says no.
Go.
"Me and my cousin gonna be okay."

Maybe.
Maybe not.

I turn and face the ocean.
Swallow what keeps trying to come up.
Closing my eyes
I tell Sister
"I'm not sure I can do it."

She says what Lottie Jean says.
I can do anything.

He squeaks.

I freeze.

Titus comes up to me
hopping on his good foot.

Sister steps in front of me.
I step aside
get so dizzy I could faint.

Breathing in deep
I look at my feet.
Think about Daddy.
Me standing in his shoes.

"What you want, Titus?"

He almost looks shy when he says,
"Your ma was the best teacher I ever had.
The only one to say
that learning wasn't no foreigner to me."

Sounds like Ma.

"I miss her."

Me too.

"I been mad at you ever since Dog passed
and your mother almost left us."

Me too.

"But after what you done for me today, I took it as a sign"—

    Ma believed in those—

"to leave you be. Try to anyhow.
Because your ma always expected better of me."

BIG SURPRISE

It's a surprise to me too
when I hand Titus Baker my helmet.

"I did a lot of thinking in it.
Had a lot of fun.

Ma would want you to have it."

His eyes get wide.
His fingers fiddle
while he tells me what I already know.
Ma's situation got his dad to thinking
changing.
So, he put Titus in school again.

"Go on, Titus. Take it."
Red reaches for the helmet.

Titus slaps his hand away.

"It's mine. Ain't it?"
His eyes go from mine to Red's
to mine again.

I nod my head.
Yes.

You'd think he was taking
one of Hattie's birds out my hand
he's so careful.
Then
out of nowhere they show up.

Sister and me wave
half expecting the widows to say for us to head home with them
right now instantly.
That Gran is crying a river over us.

"Them that's coming, come," is all Miss Mamie says.

Without a goodbye
good luck
or thank you very much
he's off
walking with Red up to the wagon.

I half expect my helmet to hit the ground.
Only it doesn't.
It goes on his head.

MA KNEW

The moon
the sky and the planets belong to everyone.
Ma always said that.

But the beach is divided up
so we stay on our side
where the lighthouse is
and a Ferris wheel
          none too high
plus cottages far off
all built by men from our side of town.

WHERE THE TROUBLE BEGAN

Tall
standing
in a sea of grass
the lighthouse looks at the ocean
looks after sailors
ships
and boats.
A star
it lights up the night
the ocean too
erasing the blue in spots
sounding
a foghorn
a warning
when storms of trouble come.

But when Ma lost her footing
and fell in the water

it just stood there
like me.

THE ATLANTIC

The ocean
comes and goes
grabbing the shore with it.

TATTOOS

Footprints
behind us
tattoos in the sand
show where we've been

where we're going.

Lottie grins
runs ahead to be with Sister and her birds.

I keep my eyes on the lighthouse.
Think about Ma running up all those steps
not hurt or sick or gone from us for months.

WHAT DADDY WROTE

Hattie runs faster than I've seen her
in a long while.

Getting on the boulder isn't easy.
It takes her three tries to climb up
walk to the edge and sit down.

I tear up some.
Lottie Jean asks what's the matter.

"We sat on this rock
every time we came," Sister tells her.

Sister reaches down
helps us up.

"See."
She points.

Daddy dug Ma's initials in the rock.
The first time they came here
he proposed.

She said yes.

ONLY ME AND MA

I talk and talk
for no reason I can think of
except nerves
and me wanting to keep my brain busy
thinking on something else.

"How big is the moon?" I ask Sister.
     She smiles when she answers.
"About two thousand miles wide."

     One day I'll walk on it. I promised Ma.

"How many people are there on our planet?"

I whisper the answer when they don't know.
     "Two billion or so."

I let a breath out.
Watch the waves come in
go out.
Hold my breath again.

"Does it snow in Iceland?"
     I laugh at Lottie's question.

"Do people shed skin?"

Sister and Lottie argue
     try to prove how much they know.

But only I know what happened to Ma.

TRUE FRIENDS

Lottie stares at the moon.
Says she thought it would surely be blue.

Me and Sister laugh
hold on tight.

Eyes closed
Lottie Jean makes a wish.
Asks the moon to take her bad luck and bury it.

Just as quick
she asks if she seems any different.

Hattie's eyes widen.
"You've been nothing but kind to me, Lottie Jean.
A good-luck charm."

Sister brings up Lottie's bright smile and caring ways.
Then thanks her for her kindnesses.

"I hardly had a single friend before you showed up."

"Kindness is its own good luck. Plant it and it'll grow."
Lottie says her grandmother taught her that.
But with so much bad luck
she says she never much believed her.

Sister smiles.
"Well, you grew yourself a friend. Two."

ALL ALONE

The lighthouse has almost a hundred steps
each shaped like a slice of pie turned sideways
made from Carolina pine trees.

Those narrow steps mean
you walk up on your feet
come down on your backside.

I didn't mind.
Ma either.
We laughed all the way to the bottom most times.

But that night I was by myself.

NO MORE EXCUSES

"I tried to save her, Hattie."

Knees up
barefooted on the warm rock
Sister stares at the moon.

My eyes find the ocean
calm
not like it was the day
Ma
went in with me close behind.

Sister stands.
Hands me her hand.
"It's time, James Henry."

"I . . . I . . . I . . ."

"Let it out, James Henry. Tell it all."

I look at the lighthouse.
"It's our secret," Ma told me that night.

ME

I knew better
than to go to the lighthouse alone.

But I was mad at Ma.

SISTER'S TEARS

All the drops of water in the ocean
couldn't add up to the tears I cried over Dog and Ma.
Nor the ones me and Sister share sitting here.

THE TRUTH LITTLE BY LITTLE

Sometimes
　　Ma doesn't notice anything.
Like how mad I was at her that night
because of those Bakers.

It was *their* papers she was grading.
Them she was thinking of
　　getting things ready for a meeting with their daddy.
Ma wanted to prove they had what it took to excel in school
to create a different life than the one they were being handed.

"Which means we cannot go tonight, James Henry.
Perhaps another time," she said,
like the moon sets its clock by us.

She was still at the schoolhouse when I ran away
I tell Sister for the first time.

A REGULAR MOTHER

Sister stands and stares
lets the water kiss her feet.
I stay on dry sand.

"I miss her something awful.
But I'm awfully mad at her too,"
she says.

Sister thinks she tucked it away
all the mad and sad she felt when it came to Ma.

"Ma got you the birds," I say.

Hattie smiles.

"Birds? Sugar, why?" Daddy said
the first time Ma brought one in the house.

"James Henry has his stars.
Hattie needs something to call her own."

Ma sat on the floor cross-legged
feeding water to a bird through a dropper.

Not long after, Hattie had eleven more doves.

"There's always enough love to go around," Ma would say.

I look at Lottie skipping rocks in the ocean.

"Sister?"

"Yes, Brother."

"Did it bother you how Ma was?"

Hattie takes a while to answer.
"I just wanted
a plain ordinary
regular everyday mother . . . till we almost lost her."

She asks if it bothered me.
"All the things she did . . .
    tree sitting
    stargazing
    singing math lessons?"

I take Hattie's hand.
Say what Gran always said to us.
Ain't no two leaves alike. People either.

"Besides, we had fun, didn't we?" I ask.

She thinks on it some.
Nods. "More fun than anybody, colored or white."

In a whisper, Hattie Mae apologizes.
Says maybe her wanting to go away to school
was her wanting to leave all her troubles behind
me included
along with Ma and her illness
the South and its ways.

She eyes the moon.
Twists her head this way and that

like it'll help her see better
   when the moon is practically filling up the sky tonight.

"Maybe a blue moon doesn't do anything at all, James Henry,
except brighten the sky.
And it's us who have to fix what needs fixing."

NOW OR NEVER

For the first time
I tell Hattie everything.

I have to
I see

or it will always be in me locked tight.
A boogeyman

scaring me.

MA, ME, AND THE MOON

I walked to the top of the lighthouse that night.

Went to the lantern room
where the light shines out onto the ocean.

Caught my breath.
Went outside onto the widow's walk
which circles the top of the lighthouse like a brim circles a hat.

I missed Ma.
Up there we spotted the constellations
looked at planets with our bare eyes
talked about how far space went
and me
full-grown
an astronomer
a wish she had for herself once.

But it was just me watching the moon that night
the moon watching the ocean and everything in it
the lightkeeper watching out for ships and boats
and boys who ought to know better
till he fell asleep.

By the time Ma showed up
I was sitting on the beach
under the moon with Dog.

"Tonight is our secret," she said.

BEFORE EVERYTHING CHANGED

"We'll tell everyone it was my idea to come here."
She came in Uncle's truck.

Ma's hand was in mine
till Dog came to her with a stick in his mouth.

Laughing
running back and forth in the sand
we played fetch under the moon.
till my pants and
the bottom of her skirt were as wet as our feet.

"Daddy didn't know where you were," Hattie says.
"Nobody did."

"Your father won't like it," Ma told me.
"You running off
me rewarding you for it."

 "Oh, James Henry," Lottie Jean says.
 Sister holds on to my hand.

"I threw the stick too far.
Dog went after it anyhow.
Ma went after Dog.

I ain't see 'em after a while.
Ma didn't answer when I called.
I tried to be brave, Hattie.
I went into the water after her.
Got her to her knees.
Helped her to her feet."

I remember holding on to Ma.
Her holding on to me.
Us heading for the beach.
Dog in the water crying.

"She went back for him, Hattie.
And it's all my fault.
If I had done what Ma said
all the bad that happened that night
would never have happened."

Sister kisses my cheek.

"Can't you see, James Henry,
helping Ma the way you did made you brave?
No matter how the day ended."

I think on it some.

"You really are a hero, James Henry," Lottie says.
"And brave besides."

She conjures up our time in Reign Forest.
The food I found for them
me tending to Titus Baker's foot
helping her and Sister be brave
        when it seemed as if all their courage had run out.

With my head turned sideways
        I stare up at the moon
        and think of Ma
        the bravest of us all.

Then for her sake
I walk up to the water's edge
dip my toes in.

BECAUSE OF THE BLUE MOON

"Don't you feel it, James Henry?"
Lottie asks.

I don't know what she's talking about.

"I feel it."
Up she jumps.
Spinning like a top.
"Our luck changing."

The ocean spits on us.

Sister and me follow Lottie.
Turn in circles
our arms stuck out like wings.

"I do feel something," I say, stopping.

Closing my eyes, I see Ma running again.
Winning.
Swimming back to us.
Dog racing up to me.
Licking my toes
like he did all those times
forgiving me.

"Let's go home," Sister says.

Looking back at the lighthouse, I nod
take a few steps
then change my mind.

MA'S FRIEND

The lightkeeper never had a wife
nor kids of his own.
Me and Ma was always good company
he told us more than once.
He's old as the salt in the sea, seems like.
Toothless.
Always grinning.
But not the day Daddy took us back
to put flowers on the water for Dog.

That day
Old Jim looked up at the sky.
Told us the name of Ma's favorite
planet
like we didn't know.

"I miss her," he said.
"She was a breath of fresh air.
Dog too. Let her know I asked about her
tell her I'm as sorry as I can be."

Before we knew it
he was gone.
Headed to the lighthouse
with his new assistant lightkeeper,
Hardy Jefferson,
Ma's favorite student ever
besides me.
Hired after her accident
by the lightkeeper
who told Dad it was the least he could do.

THE RACE

Lottie Jean, me, and Sister

sneak past the lightkeeper's house.

"All those steps?"
Lottie leans low and stares up to the top.

"I couldn't possibly," she says.

Sister shakes her head no.
"It's damp in here.
With cobwebs in the corners.
Poor lighting besides."

But we three race up the steps anyhow.

Our feet echo.
Our words float up and bounce down.
Passing Sister and Lottie
I see Ma smiling
hear her clap and cheer
with Dog beside her wagging his tail.

We three run the race Ma never could
with me far ahead
　　　winning when it's over.

Hattie comes in second place.
Lottie gave up
　　　for the sake of her hair, she said.

Sister and me end up on the widow's walk.

"I'm lucky to have you for a brother."
She puts her arm over my shoulder.
Brings up Gran
says
it's time for us to head home.

Before I know it
she's sitting on the steps
making her way down.

I stay put
keep my eyes on that blue moon
howl for Dog's sake.

LEAVING THE LIGHTHOUSE

"Who's that?"
Lottie asks, looking back.

It's Old Jim
on the other side
of the widow's walk
with his long white beard
    short white hair
    brown skin
wrinkled from salt and old age.

He waves. We do too.

On our way to the steps
I free a dragonfly from Sister's hair
spy a grasshopper on my shoulder
smile
and smile
and smile.
Lottie asks about him.

Old Jim could read the sea
but didn't know his ABCs.

Ma figured it out
not long after we got here.
He was buying pliers at the hardware store.
She needed a new comb.

It wasn't easy.
Didn't happen overnight either.
But she made a deal with him.
Taught him to read in secret.

He paid her in sand and moonlight.
Let us picnic with the crabs and jellyfish
dance in the waves
read under a full moon
once a month only
after the beach closed.
And the crowds were gone.

Each time
Ma climbed those steps to the top.
It's all she wanted as a child, she'd say.
But the last lightkeeper always told her no.
Old Jim should of sent me home
the night I showed up on my own
he told me so later.
"But for your ma's sake
I let you stay."

He regretted it.

I push away the sadness,
'cause it's been a while
since I walked outside
stepped foot on the beach
ran up those lighthouse steps.

Outside, I smile
and smile
and smile some more.

Lottie ask if I'm okay.

"I'm fine. Just fine. Great."

AN UNEXPECTED GUEST

No sooner does Hattie start hitching a ride
does a car drive by on the opposite side
turns around quick
comes to a stop where we are.

One good look at the driver

and for sure
we know we're in trouble.

HOME AGAIN

Uncle a nagging tooth
that even the dentist couldn't pull.
Steps out the car
his voice thundering.

"Get over here, boy."

I look at the moon 238,855
    miles away
instead of him.
Ma taught me that.
"You can visit it in your head
anytime down here is a bother."

"Boy!" Uncle hollers again.
"Didn't you learn no lessons?
Don't you remember that ocean almost took you from us?"
His voice shakes.
Goes from mad to something else.

"Your gran . . ."
He clears his throat. His eyes stay on mine till I look away.
". . . is home worried sick thinking . . ."

I ask if he hates me.

"Hate?"
He leans against the car.
"I thought maybe the Klan got you
or the ocean won this time."

Sister reaches up
pats his shoulder.

"We're fine, Uncle. Just fine. See?"
She shows him her teeth for some reason.
A smile as big as the hat on his head.

He laughs.
Squeezes her shoulder.
Hugs me like I've been away forever.

UNCLE'S TURN TO LET GO

In the dark,
up one road down the other
Uncle's new car never stops
never goes too fast too slow
never breaks the rules.

All the while
he talks about me and Ma
the day he found us.
Her in the ocean
jellyfish circling
biting
water in her lungs.
Me
on the sand
nose down
barely breathing
exhausted
from trying to rescue Ma.

"Twins are supposed to care for one another
from the womb on," he says.

They are.

"Protect each other."

Sure 'nuff.

"I lent her my truck.
I shoulda known better."

I wait for him to yell at me again.
He apologizes.

Lottie Jean thanks the moon.
Sister too.

Uncle tells us what we already know
he blamed everything and everyone for that night.
The lightkeeper.
Ma and me.
The ocean.
God.
"Even your father.
Women ought not be so free, I told him."

Lottie sits up.
Sister's mouth opens wide
closes shut.

"Aberdeen always was different.
Went to college, didn't she?
Even after folks said she shouldn't."
Under his breath he says
"She's
the best sister a man ever had."

He speeds up.
Slows down.
Sweats in the dark.
Pulls over to the side of the road
cries.

I do like Sister.
Pat his back and shoulder.

He rubs my head.
Says Gran
    had a good talk with him.
Reminded him that what's left sometimes
    is still a pretty good deal.
Enough to build a life with
if we open our eyes
stop looking back like that will change things.

"Family is the most important thing, hear me, boy?"

"Yes, Uncle."

"And nothing can ever separate you from me
    your mother from us.
Not trains or oceans, life or death.
Ya hear, boy?"

"Yes, Uncle."

Pulling up to the house, he stops the car once more.
Lets the girls out first.

"We did our best, you and me."

    We did.

"So let's leave what's behind us behind us."
I stop on the steps to the house.
Stare at his hand.
"Even your fingers and job?"

Uncle got gangrene from a rusty can
the night he came looking for us.

He was sure it was a crab
in the ocean
scratching him.
Picking it up
he cut himself
with the sharp raggedy edges.

His hand got infected.
He lost three fingers.
The railroad fired him.

My eyes twitch.
My lip jumps.

I apologize to Uncle again.

Tipping back his hat, he says,
"I'm still standing, ain't I, son?"

My eyes get big when I see his smile.
"You sure are, Uncle!"

He hugs me again.
I hug him back this time.

Neither one of us lets go.

OFF TO DETROIT

On the roof with my toes pointed up
and the train passing by
I think about Hattie Mae
up north since last month.

"Ready, James Henry?"
Lottie Jean walks over to me.

Lays herself down beside me.
Closes her eyes.

"You gotta feed 'em twice a day," I say.

"I know."

"If one of 'em gets lost . . ."

"Hattie left the birds to me, didn't she?"

She did.
The dentist is downstairs
        ready to take the birds to their new home.

Me, Gran, Uncle, and Daddy
        leave for Detroit in the morn.

Ma's on the mend.
Talking.
Walking with help.
Trying to remember what the ocean
        tried to make her forget.

"Don't change," Lottie Jean says.
"Or I'll be disappointed."

"I won't."

She heads for the fence
	with a few of Hattie's birds trailing behind.

"I'll miss this,"
she says, leaning over.

"Me too."

I join her.
Wish her happy birthday.

"It's the best one ever,"
	she says, calling me her good-luck charm.

Then
from under her new blue hat comes a letter.

"For me?"

"From Hattie.
It came with my birthday surprise."

Before she disappears inside the house
Lottie blows me a kiss.
Says the South truly is hospitable.
Tells me never to forget the summer we had.

How could I?

I sit in my rocket ship
    read out loud.

"Dear James Henry:

I miss you madly.
Wish you were here.
You'd love Philadelphia
you really would.

But at least we'll be closer.
And I'll get to visit Gran while she's in Detroit.

Guess what?
I have a surprise for you.
On your behalf
I wrote Buck Rogers
explained everything.

I told him about our adventures.
Let him know there is no better brother
    no better friend or space explorer than you, James Henry.
And even though the contest is over
I wanted him to know your name
how brave and courageous you are.
    Wouldn't it be wonderful if someone named a star after you
    or Ma?

I love you, Brother,
to the moon and back
to the ocean deep
to the edge of the earth
to the furthest galaxy.
And I can't wait to see you.

Your forever twin,
Hattie Mae
Captain every now and then.

Sharon G. Flake and her father.

AUTHOR'S NOTE

Several years ago, my dad told me a story that I haven't been able to forget. As an elementary school student at the Negro Normal School in North Carolina, he loved to gaze out of his classroom window up at the sky. He was, on more than one occasion, told by his teacher to return to his studies. I was curious as to what caught my dad's attention. It turns out it was the sky, the stars, the planets. He'd sit in class daydreaming about them.

My father's response prompted me to ask him a question: "What career would you have chosen if you had grown up in a different era?" Dad's reply floored me. He would have been an astronomer, he told me. At the writing of this book, my dad is ninety-six. He grew up under Jim Crow laws, which legalized racial segregation and discrimination. Yet no person or system could contain his curiosity, thirst for information and knowledge, or ability to dream a different life for himself. This book would not exist if not for him.

James Henry, the protagonist of my novel, is named after my dad and his brother, whom I've never met. I wanted to honor them each by doing so. James Henry, like my dad, is a seeker, with his eyes forever on the universe and all that it contains. When something goes wrong, he becomes housebound of his own accord. With the encouragement of his sister, James Henry must find his own way out.

Once in a Blue Moon takes place in fictional Seed County, North Carolina. My father grew up in Anson County. Most of my life, he spoke of the one-room schoolhouse he attended, the train that ran by his one-room home, their family garden, his dad. He lovingly spoke about his grandmother, Gran, who raised him with values he still holds dear to this day. I kept these images and Dad's love for his home tucked in my heart as I wrote. I did turn to resources at the library and elsewhere when it came to astronomy, norms of the day, and the agriculture and wildlife of North Carolina. But in creating a fictional town, I was able to create a world that I would have wished for my father, while including aspects of a world and society that I hope shall remain in the past. For example, beaches during this era were often segregated. It was typical for African Americans to be relegated to ones in hazardous condition or far away from their homes. A few beach resorts were owned and operated by African Americans. I have given James Henry and their community their own beach, along with a lighthouse. Lighthouses, for some reason, have attracted my attention for years now. Everyone should have access to one, I believe, and James Henry and his family are no different.

In this book, readers will also find a tribute of sorts to my mother Roberta's side of the family. The character Titus was named after my great-grandfather.

People often ask how I became an author. I always give the same answer: it's because of my dad; my mother, Roberta; and my uncles and aunts. They sat around our kitchen table many a day, telling stories about our family, their communities, the country.

So often they laughed out loud, using sound effects or imitating the voices of the folks they spoke of. They were my very first storytellers. The ones who helped me understand how important and necessary stories are to our very survival. James Henry would have loved my father. He and Dad together speak volumes about what is possible when we dare to open ourselves up to the world—and when the world dares to make space for us.

SHARON G. FLAKE